Diana Gray

Mannie Fuego's Guide to Good Eats

The zombie apocalypse never tasted so good.

Mannie Fuego's Guide to Good Eats

by Diana Gray

Editor: Kelly Scriven

Diana Gray
P.O. Box 1193
Ukiah, CA 95482

RobotsAndMagicConsulting@gmail.com

RobotsAndMagic.com

To my Stellar Companion, Jack, who never stopped believing in this story. Wait, how did I not manage to work a Journey reference into this thing? I bet Mannie Fuego loves Journey.

In seriousness, I don't know if I ever laughed harder than when I was writing this book and howling at the absurdities with you. Can't wait to do it all again when I sit down to pen the sequel.

And, hey, here's another dedication because it's my book and I can do whatever I want on this page:

To anyone who has ever had trouble finding their way.

Chapters

CHAPTER ONE

A Small Town in Northern California

If we want to get technical, it all started with a potato. Well, a sack of potatoes.

Until recently, I was working as a fry cook at my uncle's restaurant. And really, 'restaurant' is a nice term for greasy dive burger joint. We were a rambling, sweaty shack of health code violations, but it paid the bills, and I didn't finish high school, so it's not like my career outlook was all that great. Plus, necromancy isn't exactly a marketable skill. It's definitely not something you put on your LinkedIn profile.

I meant to do more with my life. I really, really did. I was an honor student, always in or at least near the top of my class. I wasn't the guy who won geography bees, but I did get good grades and was at a college reading level before I finished middle school. I didn't know exactly what I wanted to be when I grew up, but I knew I had options.

I started cutting class in high school, just after my biology class started us in on dissecting cats. I shit you not, we leapfrogged right over amphibians and went straight to mammals. It was fucking sick. The room smelled like formaldehyde, and we spent an hour a day for two months pulling dead cats apart bit. By. Bit. Or, we were supposed to. I lasted exactly five minutes into day one.

Mom was so excited when I told her what happened. "The Gift" often skips a generation, and she was always so disappointed that she couldn't follow in my grandpa's footsteps. I'm not one hundred percent clear on what exactly Pop-pop was up to with his gift, but I'm pretty sure it involved some clandestine dealings with a handful of oddball "religious groups" (I hesitate to call them cults—I really don't have enough information here) throughout the years. Pop-pop swears that he never really tampered with the rules of the universe when he was doing this work, but that certainly didn't stop him from taking money from anyone who wanted to glimpse the other side of the mortal veil (including the fine folks over at the local Church of Satan).

Karma got Pop-pop in the end, though. See, being a necromancer, Pop-pop had it in his head that he was going to live forever, at least in a sense. He set it up so that when he died, his shade would stick around with us in a harmless inanimate object, like an urn or something. Unfortunately, he miscast his spell and ended up in the armchair a few years ago. It's not so bad, I guess, but suffice it to say we don't have company over that often.

Anyway, as you can likely guess, I discovered "The Gift" in biology. Being on an advanced academic track, I ended up in biology class as a freshman and moved on to advanced bio when I was a sophomore. Unfortunately, a significant portion of the advanced bio class involved dissection labs, which ... is just gross. I'm sorry to any science lovers who may be reading this, but I'm really fucking squeamish.

So, the fateful day came, and there I was in my big rubber apron, staring down at the very dead cat my teacher had plunked down in front of me. I mustered all of my courage to touch the disgusting thing and—I shit you not—when my fingers just barely brushed the goddamn cat, it blinked. Then, as if the blink wasn't horrifying enough, the cat lifted its head and looked at me. I was out of there. I ran all the way home with my apron and latex gloves still on.

After the incident in bio, I started quietly picking up shifts at Uncle Bernie's burger joint. Mom was home on disability; she has pretty intense agoraphobia, so it was easy to hide my activities from her at first. So long as I left with a backpack in the morning and came home in time for dinner, she didn't ask questions. When she finally realized I had dropped out of school, she didn't say anything. I started buying groceries, picking up things we needed around the house, paying rent. I guess we're not very good at having tough conversations.

The one good thing about "The Gift" is this odd little talent I discovered a few years ago. You see, Uncle Bernie's place used to operate on a shoestring budget, so the produce often came to us looking a little worse for wear. But one touch of my profane magic and the potatoes were like new! And it doesn't just work on potatoes. I got so into it, I started experimenting with all kinds of produce. I can make soft, mealy tomatoes vine-ripe again, work the bug holes out of peaches ... the only thing I don't mess with anymore is pineapples (long story). These days, if our produce delivery includes wilted romaine or moldy onions, Uncle Bernie just tosses them my way and poof: they're farm fresh. Over time, we've gotten a pretty good reputation for having the freshest fries in town. Business has picked up, slow but steady.

So the other day, Uncle Bernie came in with fifty pounds of this fancy Wagyu beef. He was psyched. He got a hot tip that a famous Food Network guy was coming to shoot a little TV spot: Mannie Goddamn Fuego. I know, we were pumped. I mean, I'm not Mannie's biggest fan—actually, I think Mannie Fuego is an obnoxious douchebag—but TV! So Uncle Bernie was thinking he could invest in some fancy meat and we'd get a good review, business would get a boost, you get the idea.

It's actually my fault things went wrong. I tripped the breaker, and I guess the fridge lost power last night. I didn't think it would be a big deal to give the beef a little boost. I'd never tried my powers on meat before, but what's the harm, right? I mean, one minute it smelled like shit, the next it's fresh as ... Well, not a daisy, but you get the idea.

Things went pretty great at first. Mannie Fuego swaggered in at high noon, his spiked fire-engine red hair glistening in the neon lights. He caused a scene with his camera crew, did an interview with Uncle Bernie, and raved into the camera about the fresh, fancy beef and tasty french fries. I could hear them in the back as I freshened up the produce delivery. Sadly, even the expensive new produce people still gave us a bruiser here and there. Still, there was something kind of fun about wiping the brown spots out, watching the ugliness melt out of them. I know it's just vegetables, but there's something kind of poetic about it.

Despite all of the excitement leading up to his visit, I didn't go out to meet Mannie myself. I preferred to stay in the back and work, and I was kind of relieved when the crew packed up their bus and rolled away. Mannie took the bustle and excitement with him, and people started to file out of our little burger joint as the celebrity glow rapidly faded from our corner of town.

Anyway, I noticed something was off about two hours after Uncle Bernie's lunch break. He eats a burger just about every day, and it shows ... in a bad way. He's got a gut, and his health is just bad. But today, Uncle Bernie's signature wheeze was ... Well, it was more like a groan. I went to the back room to check on him and ... Look, I know this sounds insane, but he was dead. Or, rather, undead. Thankfully, Uncle Bernie wasn't a fast guy to begin with, and I managed to close him away in the back room before he could take a bite out of me.

Necromancers have a long, proud history of raising the dead and tampering with the afterlife for a whole host of reasons. I can definitively say that I am the first to cause this particular effect via tainted hamburgers.

So, I know zombie lore, and I get that I was supposed to shed a tear and off Uncle Bernie with a blunt object. But I couldn't. I don't like death, or blood, or any of it. I like to think of myself as a pacifist, though Pop-pop would tell you I'm just a big soft-hearted wimp like my dad. And, regardless of my feelings around violence and death, I have a soft spot for Uncle Bernie. So, I locked him in the back room and left a note should anyone think to go fiddling with locked doors while I'm away. I thanked my lucky stars that the restaurant was empty—caught in that mid-afternoon slump between the late lunchers and Early Bird Special crowd. Heart pounding, I flipped the "CLOSED" sign as I bolted out of the diner and gunned the engine on my Dodge Colt so fast I almost killed the old girl.

Now, driving through town, I know I've fucked up. Zombies are already everywhere. I narrowly miss hitting a zombie toddler as I cross Main Street. I'm starting to regret all of the business we got at lunch.

The town I grew up in can best be described with three words: small, rural, boring. When I was born, the town had one stoplight, and I distinctly remember it being a big deal when we got the second one. Unfortunately, it is this very small-town charm that seems to have doomed my neighbors. Just about everyone heard about Mannie Fuego coming to Uncle Bernie's today, which means that—no exaggeration—about half the town came by the restaurant today to grab a bite. Most of the zombie action is in the middle of town, but by the time I make it home, plenty are starting to swarm my little neighborhood.

For the first time in a long time, I'm grateful that mom is an agoraphobe and has been locked inside all day. I nearly crash my car into the garage door as I scream into the driveway. Kicking the driver's side door shut, I scramble up to the front porch, keys at the ready in one sweaty, shaking hand. It takes more effort than it should to jam the key into the lock and swing the door open. Safely on the other side, I throw the door closed and lean back against it to catch my breath.

"Bradley?" Mom calls from the next room. She practically has to shout to be heard over the TV. "You're home early."

Our house is a pretty standard little suburban family home: three bedrooms upstairs; kitchen, living room, and front entryway downstairs; plus a handful of bathrooms. For all that Mom never leaves, she does keep the place tidy. Dad used to be the one who kept house, but after he passed, my mom took up the mantle. She actually makes a habit of cleaning every day—I think it's good for her anxiety.

"Hey Mom," I call back, sliding the deadbolt before I venture into the living room.

Mom is on the couch working on some knitting as the TV drones incessantly from the other side of the room. Pop-pop's in his usual spot beside the couch. (We typically only ever move him when we need to do the annual carpet cleaning.) Before I can get my thoughts straight, Mannie Fuego's voice cuts through my consciousness.

"HEY FOLKS, HERE WE ARE IN SAINT LOUIS, MISSOURI, CHECKIN' OUT THE—"

"Mom, can you maybe—"

Pop-pop interjects, "OH FOR CHRISSAKE, SARAH, TURN DOWN THE GODDAMN TV—"

"Dad, you're the one constantly complaining you can't hear—"

Mom and Pop-pop start to go at it and, as my mind buzzes with barely-contained panic, it's all I can do to just stare at Mannie Fuego on TV. Excited as I was to have Uncle Bernie's place get a spotlight on a big national show, I do wish it had been someone cooler than Mannie Fuego. Mannie's whole schtick is being this over-the-top everyman type who just loves a good burger. Everything about him rubs me the wrong way: his stupid hair, his insistence on wearing sunglasses inside, his slack-jawed grin. He's never got anything intelligent to say, just gets by on his aging frat-boy lingo and inexplicable charm.

Fed up, I snatch the remote from my mom's hand and turn the TV off.

"Bradley," Mom admonishes.

"I'm sorry, but you have to listen to me. We don't have much time."

I explain everything. The potato trick, the Wagyu beef I tried to freshen up, Uncle Bernie. Pop-pop perks up and starts asking questions. The way he's acting, I start to wonder if maybe he's proud. Of course, my hopes are dashed when he finally concludes, "Son, you've fucked up real good."

"Cool, thanks Pop-pop."

"Dad," my mom chides. "You must know a way to put a stop to this."

Pop-pop grumbles for a minute. Were he not an armchair, I imagine he'd be leaning back and folding his arms as he thinks. He makes a sound like he's clearing his throat (which honest to God always confuses the ever-loving hell out of me) and sighs. "There's only one way to turn this around. You gotta stop the first zombie you turned."

Of course, I know who that is. The first person to eat the tainted Wagyu beef was none other than the infamous Mannie Fuego.

So, after a great deal of arguing and Pop-pop putting his foot down, the three of us are driving around town in Mom's ancient blue Chevy. Mom's at the wheel, and I'm in the truck bed with Pop-pop, who insisted on coming. It's going to be a long fucking day, and when it's finally over, I may look into vocational school or something. I can't possibly do any harm as a carpenter, right?

$$\star \; \star \; \star$$

Mannie Fuego is hungry. He is hungrier than he can ever remember being. But nothing satisfies his palate. He's craving something ... new. And as he rides in the back of his tour bus through the sleepy small town, he finds that none of the usual fare in his cupboards is doing the trick.

When they stop off in the next city, Mannie finally understands. The tour bus driver ambles to the back to take a leak, and Mannie Fuego ambles to the tour bus driver to take a lick. At first, Bob (Mannie thinks his name is Bob, but he isn't sure anymore) thinks Mannie is just being a goofball and goes along with it.

"Real funny, big guy," Bob jests.

CHAPTER TWO

Skipping Town

Mom has the same Bob Dylan song on repeat, and by the fifteenth time I have to hear him warble "Positively 4th Street," I'm ready to scream.

Huddled up in the bed of the truck next to Pop-Pop, I readjust my sweaty grip on my old metal baseball bat and nudge a particularly bothersome zombie away from me. To my great relief, they don't seem like they can run, and their motor functions are pretty jerky. A lot of them are trapped inside buildings on Main Street, and the ones ambling around out here don't seem particularly ravenous or violent. Mostly, they look confused.

Bob Dylan breaks through my reverie, "You see me on the street, you always act surprised—"

"Mom," I holler through the rear window's dusty screen, "do you think maybe we could quit with the music for a while? Or at least change the song?" I rethink that. No more Bob Dylan. "Scratch that, just—"

My request is interrupted by a hard bump, and I'm sent sprawling into the truck bed. Using Pop-Pop to pick myself back up and peeling a leaf from my face, I bluster, "The fuck was that?"

"Bradley, language!" Mom hisses.

I can almost feel Pop-pop roll his eyes along with me.

"Sorry, Mother. What obstacle in yonder road did send me flying into yon truck bed?"

"Okay, now you're just being a smart alec."

"Mom!"

I can feel Mom cringe as she admits, "I think it was another one of your classmates. Sorry, honey!"

We've doubled back towards Bernie's, where the bulk of the zombies are concentrated. Mom's done three loops around town—in a weird way she seems to be enjoying the drive. It's a nice day, after all. Just a few too many zombies out and about for my taste. I stifle a nervous giggle as I spot two trying to climb a tree to—presumably—eat the pair of aggravated squirrels who've scampered to the higher branches. I half hope they'll start pelting the zombies with acorns, but Mom turns a corner before I can see more.

Settling back down next to Pop-pop, I reach for my phone reflexively and mutter, "This is so fucking stupid. Three hours driving around this fucking place and nothing."

Pop-Pop speaks up. "You sure he's still in town?"

My stomach knots. This isn't something I had considered, but of course Mannie Fucking Fuego wouldn't bother to stay in this shithole. He's rich, he can go anywhere! Besides, San Francisco is an hour and a half down the freeway. He probably set a course for the city the second they wrapped filming at Uncle Bernie's!

Still, that's an educated guess at best, and San Francisco is a big place to be combing for one douchebag celebrity chef turned zombie.

"Well, no," I finally admit, absently scrolling through my Facebook feed.

Over the years, my Facebook connections have shaken out into one of three tiers: friends, people I still pretend to be friends with despite the fact that I haven't seen or spoken to them in years, and people I met once and for some reason felt compelled to cement said meeting with a lifelong digital connection. Reading all of the generally inane bullshit these three distinct groups of people have put up on Facebook today, the gravity of the situation I've created starts to hit me. Whether I like or care about them at all, each and every one of these people could die. That one guy from the school newspaper got married yesterday. Today, he could be a zombie, because my dumb ass decided to fancy up some beef. Because I'm a fuckup. And now this genuinely nice guy I worked on the school newspaper with (and probably his cute new husband) are going to be zombies, and it's all my fault.

"Fuck, fuck, fuck," I whisper through a fresh haze of tears, still compulsively scrolling through my Facebook feed. It's all I can do. It's grounding and normal and stupid.

"It's okay sweetie, we'll keep looking. We'll find Emmanuel," Mom assures me as she turns back onto Main Street.

Mom loves Mannie Fuego. I mean, LOVES him. And the prospect of Mannie being at Bernie's diner almost got her out of the house today. Just nearly. This morning, she was doing positive affirmations over breakfast. She took her anxiety meds as usual and even took half a Xanax with her morning OJ. She had flashed me a little smile as I inhaled my Lucky Charms and said, "I guess I'll see you at work later," as I grabbed my keys and coat.

It kills me that she didn't make it. And even though I'm not really into him, it would've been really cool if she had gotten a chance to meet Mannie today... especially now that this whole zombie thing happened. I mean, I knew she wouldn't make it out of the house today, but I'd found myself wishing she could anyway. I guess that was foolish of me.

As I rapid-fire scroll through the never-ending deluge of memes, political rants, and selfies that make up my Facebook feed these days, something flashes by that makes my heart stop. I lift my finger from the screen and slowly roll the images back up. There, on my screen, is Mannie Fuego, that dipshit, gape-mouthed smile plastered on his face as he stands next to that girl I met at a friend's party a few months ago—Emily. Emily liked the same music as me, and for some reason I had drunkenly assumed that maybe this was the basis of a lifelong friendship. When I sobered up the next day, I hadn't really felt like unfriending her. Now I get updates about her life directly on my phone on a daily basis and—for reasons I can't explain—I bother reading them. I know things about Emily I don't even know about my real friends, all because Emily is a semi-obnoxious Facebook over-sharer.

As I stare at the picture she snapped with Mannie Fuego, though, I thank Emily for her compulsive need to let everyone know what she's up to at all times. Not only does her post have a timestamp from just five minutes ago, she's also got location settings on. She's checked in at Pier 39.

"He's in San Francisco," I say hurriedly. "We have to get to Pier 39."

"Damn kids and your phones," Pop-pop grumbles. "Guess you finally did us some good." I imagine that if Pop-pop weren't a chair, he'd sigh and resettle himself with his back against the cab before he continued, "You heard the boy, Sarah. Let's take this rig down to the city. Maybe we can get this thing finished in time to grab some crab sandwiches and get home for Survivor."

"The city?" Mom asks from the driver's seat. She's stopped at a red light for some reason, as though the bedlam around us doesn't negate traffic laws. Zombies are literally everywhere, meandering into the street, stuck in cars. A couple are even on fire for some reason.

I watch my mom through the gray crosshatching of the window screen, wondering if this will be the thing that breaks her and makes her run back to the house. Really, it was a miracle that she agreed to come at all. I think Pop-pop was the deciding factor. There's something about that stern Dad voice of his that makes everyone sit up a little straighter and consider tucking their shirts in, just for good measure.

Necromancer though he may have been, Pop-pop still has a healthy appreciation for the way life was "back in his day," when men went to work in suits and sexual harassment was called "this is just how we talk to girls, I don't see what the big deal is." Pop-pop called out every fresh piercing I came home with and definitely disapproved of my blue hair phase. Now that my blue hair phase is in its fifth year, he seems to have given up on trying to get me to dress "like a proper young man" and instead complains about other normal Grandpa things, like modern technology. All this, of course, whilst patently ignoring his reliance on modern technology to deliver a steady stream of garbage reality TV directly to his cushiony face. If he still had fingers, I'm betting Pop-pop would be using them to hold a smartphone and share memes about how his generation was superior ... because they didn't have smartphones. Ahhh, the hypocrisy of my elders.

Anyway, when Mom started to protest about staying home sick from the zombie apocalypse, Pop-pop put on his very best "I'm not having this" voice and Mom got her ass straight into the truck (after she helped me haul Pop-pop into the back, that is).

When the light turns green, Mom eases her foot onto the gas pedal, gently pushing a few errant zombies to the pavement as she makes her way through the intersection. I can't think of anything sufficient to say to her that will convince her that she'll be safer with us. I consider Googling "How to talk to your agoraphobe mom about the importance of sticking together during the zombie apocalypse," but alas...

Without warning—all right, there was some warning, because Mom always makes sure she uses the turn signal—we start heading farther away from home.

"Mom?" I ask as she makes another turn. "Where are we going?"

"The freeway, of course," she says matter-of-factly. "You'd better get in the cab and buckle your seatbelt. Oh! And don't forget to tie Pop-pop down, too. Can't have him go flying out onto the road!"

I consider saying something about how brave she's being, or even asking if she's sure, but bite my tongue. I got what I wanted; saying anything further about her decision only risks her changing her mind.

* * *

Mannie Fuego always wanted to be invited to party on a yacht spontaneously, just because. It wasn't that Mannie hadn't been on a yacht before. In fact, he had seen a total of seven and a half yacht parties in his storied career. But it was something else entirely to be spontaneously invited to join a rowdy yacht party crowd just because you're a big awesome superstar that everybody likes.

The yacht partiers spot him wandering on the pier and shout their invitations over the blaring Michael McDonald tunes. Mannie can't remember why he was at the pier in the first place, but he sure does love Michael McDonald. All Mannie really knows now (other than his love of Yacht Rock, of course) is that he is hungry, and the people on the boat look delicious. Wait, that wasn't right. Or was it?

Wandering onto the gangplank, Mannie feels his jaw drop open, and he hopes that he's smiling. It's getting hard to make any of those faces that tell people how you're feeling, so he decides that tilting his head to an extreme angle might help. A portly man wearing a captain's hat greets Mannie as he steps onto the boat.

"Mannie Fuckin' Fuego, you been smokin' the ganja my friend? You look high as fuck!"

Mannie is having a hard time understanding the man, but the soothing music beckons him in and sets his mind at ease. The man in the captain's hat ushers him further into the party and mentions making Mannie a special meal. Hearing that, everyone on the boat yells, "Let's get on the tasty train!"

Mannie likes that very much.

C HAPTER T HREE

Pier 39:
San Francisco, California

T here, that's his bus! Pull over."

Mom tuts. "Bradley, that's a loading zone, I'm going to circle around to the garage."

I consider just saying "fuck it" and jumping out of the truck but refrain for the sake of Mom's delicate nerves. So I sit on my hands and try not to vibrate out of my skin with anticipation as we slowly roll around the block and ascend five stories of concrete parking garage. Mom has to back out and into the parking spot no less than four times before she finally kills the engine. I've got the door open and my body is halfway out of the truck before I realize that neither she nor Pop-pop will be coming with me.

Mom's looking wistfully around, but it's difficult to tell what she's really thinking. I mean, is she terrified? Or relieved to finally be out of the house? Probably a little of both, if I'm honest. Sometimes I wonder about Mom's agoraphobia—not the reality of it, but the scope and severity. I hate to even admit it, but sometimes I've wondered if she uses it as an excuse to stay home and watch dreck TV all day. I mean, hey, if I could sit at home and play video games all day, I'd surely do it. It's not like my life outside of the house is anything special anyway.

But no. I know that Mom loved her job. When she finally had to take a leave of absence, she made no buts about trying to get better. But … well … she just didn't. She got worse. I'm sure there's a lot she misses about going out, trips to San Francisco maybe chief among them. We can't see much of the pier from our vantage point in the concrete parking monstrosity, but it's certainly more than she's seen in years.

"Um," I start. Stepping out onto the pavement, I consider what I ought to say. "I'll be back in a minute, I guess."

Mom nods, a wobbly smile hanging around her lips. I close the door, hoping she'll be okay while I'm gone.

As I pass by the back of the truck, Pop-pop asks, "Know how you're going to kill that son of a bitch when you find him?"

I halt, running a hand through my hair. I'd been so focused on finding Mannie, I hadn't given much thought to how I'd stop him. "About that. Isn't there some kind of spell or…?"

"No spells, son. Blunt trauma to the brain. Bullets are best. Don't suppose you've got a gun on ya?"

"Um … no, Pop-pop." I reach into the back of the truck and grab the metal baseball bat I had nabbed in my rush to get out of the house. "I suppose this will have to do?"

If Pop-pop had a face, I know he'd be frowning. Not deeply, like someone who's really upset, but really just a touch away from having a neutral expression. Clearing his throat, he finally says, "Be a lot cleaner if you had a gun."

"Noted, thanks Pop-pop," I say, starting off.

"And Bradley?"

I stop and turn. "Yeah, Pop-pop?"

"Be careful. You're the only one who can stop this from getting really out of control."

Great.

"Thanks."

As I make my way out of the parking garage and back toward the bustle of the pier, I try my best to mentally prepare myself to kill someone—really kill someone. I get upset squishing large insects, so it's hard to wrap my head around what it'll be like to swing a metal bat at Mannie Fuego's spiky red head and crunch through his skull. How many times am I going to have to hit him before he's dead?

This may seem especially weird since I come from a family of necromancers, but nothing about death sits right with me. It's just weird how something or someone can be alive and fine one minute, then dead and gone the next. It's the 'gone' part that never really made sense to me. I mean, Pop-pop is still 'here' even though his body is 'gone' … which leads me to wonder: is Mannie still 'here' since his body is still moving around? Or is he 'gone'? Either way, I don't ever want to be the one responsible for a person or creature being in the 'gone' column. You know, now that I think about it, I should probably stop eating meat.

One thing at a time, Brad.

I move as nonchalantly as I can, far too aware of the metal bat I'm toting. Still, as I meld into the throngs of slow-moving tourists, no one seems to take much notice. Seems weird to see everyone acting so normal after the bedlam we left behind in my hometown. Here, everyone's caught up in the business of Pier 39, which, if you've never seen it before and aren't hunting an undead Food Network star, is too full of distractions to make you bother with a blue-haired kid with a baseball bat. I know I probably come off as too cool for school most of the time, but I can genuinely say that the pier is a fun place to be. Regardless of what you're into, it's got something to keep you entertained. I imagine that's what brings so many people to this place day in and day out.

For my part, the pier is just as I remember it. People are clustered together watching the famous seals, lining up to go into the wax museum, forming circles around human statues and other street performers. It's so normal, I start to wonder if Mannie's tour bus was just an illusion. Cutting around an especially slow group of families with really little kids, I finally get the tour bus in my sights again. It's parked in a loading zone looking normal as can be. Staring at it, I start to wonder if my theory about what started this whole zombie debacle was totally off. I draw closer to the bus and notice something strange: a pair of feet are sticking out of some bushes just ten feet away from the tour bus's door.

Frowning, I say to myself, "Well, shit."

Peering into the bushes, I see the bloody remains of some poor, unfortunate tourist. As luck would have it, it isn't Emily—unless Emily had somehow become a middle-aged, slightly overweight man who still thought fanny packs were an acceptable thing to wear ever. His head is mostly eaten, which explains why he hasn't reanimated, and most of his portly torso has been consumed. It looked like Mannie tried to eat into the fanny pack and lost interest. Surveying the body, my stomach starts to roil.

"Fuck, this is fucking gross," I manage before the vomiting starts. It comes on without warning, and suddenly it's all I can do to keep myself upright. Puke's coming out of my mouth, my nose, and I swear there's a little bit coming out of my ears. The sheer force of it is superhuman and fucking disgusting, adding to the mess that started me puking in the first place.

When it's finally done, I'm shaking and hollow. I can't wait to find Mannie Fuego and end this so I can go home, shower, and start making something of my shitty garbage life.

Catching my breath, I'm caught off-guard by a ringtone. It's so bright and cheery, completely out of place. Luckily, it's a good foot and a half away from any blood, bones, or other gore, so I stoop to pick it up. I decline the call and, by some miracle, the phone has no passcode or thumb scan system set up. Unlocking the screen, I'm surprised to see that the phone is still open to the photo app, and what's left leaves me with a clearer narrative of what happened here.

Mannie must have stumbled off the bus in a zombified stupor but was still recognizable enough for Emily and this hapless tourist to notice him and ask for photos. As a zombie, it's unlikely that Mannie has any speech left, but it's not as if he was an eloquent or prolific speaker in life anyway. The owner of the phone I'm holding now snapped a few okay selfies with Mannie, but the images quickly turn into a grotesque slideshow. I can imagine the photo captions:

> *Me smiling with Mannie Fuego!*

> *Mannie Fuego sure seems to like me!*

> *Mannie Fuego taking a bite out of my face.*

> *Boy, if Mannie hadn't gone so quickly for my throat, I'd probably be screaming in agony. Oh, Mannie!*

> *I'm bleeding to death on the ground as a D-list celebrity eats me alive. Somehow I'm still taking pictures. Maybe my thumb is stuck on the virtual button and I'm clicking out of habit, or panic. Either way, I'm dying here on Pier 39 and no one will ever see these pictures.*

… Or something like that.

I have to give myself a bit of a pep talk to do it, but I push the rest of the dead tourist into the bushes and hope nobody else discovers this poor bastard before I can set things right.

"Sorry, dude," I mutter as I put his phone back in his fanny pack.

I head back toward Mannie's tour bus and take a look inside. Two more mostly-eaten bodies are lying among a mess of chip bags and candy bar wrappers, but there's no sign of Mannie. Stepping back off the bus, I scan the area and wonder what could possibly have happened to him. I mean, the guy's a zombie! The pier should be a horror show by now! Frustrated, I start to wander.

The sun is starting to get low in the sky, and the crowds are starting to thin as people head home or tuck into seafood dinners at overpriced restaurants. Over the quieting bustle of multilingual tourist chatter, I hear the unmistakable song chorus that every—and

I mean EVERY—American recognizes regardless of age, political leanings, or socioeconomic status. It's reverberating across the water from an obscenely large yacht. It looks like it's just set sail on one of those "tour the bay" parties people like to do for corporate celebrations and—in the in the case of our yacht rock loving music blasters—obnoxious middle-aged yuppies celebrating a 50th (or so?) birthday party.

"I BLESS THE RAIIIIINS DOWN IN AAAAFRICAAAAAAAAAAA!"

Everyone is on deck, drinking and singing along, and among them is none other than...

"Mannie!" I shout, running up the pier. My feet clatter on the old wooden boards as I dart between groups of tourists, keeping the yacht in my sight as my lungs scream for air. Reaching the tip of the pier, I'm only fifty or so feet from the boat. I climb up onto the wooden fence and bellow over the melodramatic lyrics, "HEY! MANNIE FUEGO! MANNIE FUEGO!!!"

I'm waving my arms wildly now, gesticulating like a mad man. "STOP PLEASE, THAT'S MANNIE FUEGO, I—"

"WOOOOOOOOOOOOO MANNIE FUEGO YEAH!!!" a woman shouts back in acknowledgment, which gets the whole boat going. He's smack dab in the middle of the raucous crowd, jaw hanging open in a bad facsimile of a smile. It's a miracle he hasn't eaten everyone alive by now. . .

"NO GODDAMNIT!!!" I shout, but no one hears me. The boat pulls further out into the water, and Toto fades out, leaving me hopeless and deflated. I trudge back down the quickly emptying pier, entirely unsure of what to do next, when I spot something odd ambling out of the wax museum. Several somethings, in fact.

"Fuck, really?" I mutter, making a bee-line for the small cluster of zombies. They're surprisingly docile, which makes it harder for me to go for broke and start swinging my baseball bat at them. After all, they had been innocent tourists a few hours ago. Maybe—just maybe—if I can catch back up with Mannie, I can get these people to turn back. Pop-pop seems to think that if I take out Mannie, all will be set right. I have to try, at least.

Every little noise distracts the zombies. Maybe that's what ultimately drew Mannie to the yacht? For all I know, the blaring music could have even helped calm him down. That would certainly explain why Mannie was just standing in the middle of all of those drunk rich people. I know it's stupid, but I'm compelled to start singing to them, hoping that maybe—just maybe—my dipshit plan will work.

"It's gonna take a lot to take me away from youuuuuu. . ."

All three of them look right at me, eyes as alight as they can be for dead people. Encouraged, I keep going.

"There's nothing that a hundred men or more could ever dooo. . ."

I'm cautiously walking backward toward the wax museum's door now, holding my bat aloft in case one decides to attack. Still, something about the music not only seems to be drawing their attention—it's making them docile. I swear one is smiling. Another is bobbing his head to the inaudible beat. Nearing the door, I continue.

"I bless the raaaaains down in Aaaaaafricaaaaaaaa. . ."

I'm fumbling for the handle now, other hand shakily gripping my bat as I point it at my new zombie friends. The door swings inward. I step into the wax museum and usher the zombies in. A groan behind me makes me squeal in terror.

Whirling, I smack another zombie square in the face with the bat, and it falls gracelessly to the floor. The other three I had been luring into the museum start to snarl the second I stop singing. Well, that's not quite right. Two are snarling, and one is trapped in the door. Panicking, I force my trembling lips around the all-too-familiar notes.

"Buhhh buh buh buh-buh-buh BUH!"

The zombie I've knocked over burbles happily into the carpet, while the other two stop advancing on me and resume swaying to the song. In my terror, I've managed to somehow forget everything but the chorus and the "buh buh" part of the song, so I'm forced to keep feverishly repeating them while I think about what to do. I can't just corral them into the building, can I? From what I can tell, the whole building is overrun. Hopefully it's the only one.

I know what Pop-pop would say if he was here: he'd tell me to off every single one of these zombies. And, look, I know in my heart of hearts that killing them is the logical and pragmatic thing to do. I get that. I need you to know that I get that. But if you're going to come along on this little adventure with me, you need to make your peace with the fact that I'm not really someone who does the logical and pragmatic thing most of the time. I can't kill these people, even if they're flesh-hungry undead monsters.

Sorry, Pop-pop.

I start making up new lyrics to the song as I search for one of the undead employees. When I spot one, I saunter up to him and sing, "I'm gonna haaave to steal the keeeeeys from youuuuuu."

Snatching the key ring off of the poor undead man's belt, I continue, "Not really a whole lot else that I can dooooooo."

Stepping to the doors, I hastily let myself out and sing, "I lock the zombies in the waaax museummm."

Staring at them through the glass, I sigh. "Sorry guys."

Deprived of my miserable singing voice, the zombies turn feral and bloodthirsty once again. Still, they won't be like this for long. I mean, how far can Mannie get in that yacht full of drunk assholes anyway? I'll get him tonight, turn things around, and tomorrow this will all just be a funny story.

Satisfied, my confidence is renewed, and I decide to head over to one of the overpriced restaurants to buy a round of crab sandwiches.

* * *

Mannie Fuego always dreamed of being pulled up onstage at a rock concert, just like Courteney Cox in that one Bruce Springsteen music video.

It is difficult for Mannie to recall the circumstances which led him to this concert in the first place. After leaving his delicious friends on the boat, he found himself wandering the streets. Which streets? Who knew. Passing by a building with bright, flashing lights, Mannie was drawn to the music coming from inside. To Mannie's delight, a man at the door recognized him.

"Mannie Fuckin' Fuego, hey!" the large man called. Mannie loved it when people recognized him.

"Yo Mannie," the man said as Mannie drew near, ignoring the clearly irritated line of people he was supposed to be attending to. "You want to get in and see Green Day? On the house, buddy!"

And so, Mannie found himself being ushered into an old theater and borne along the energetic crowd to the front of a frenzied mosh pit.

For the first time in hours, Mannie isn't hungry. Despite the rapid-fire beat of the music, Mannie sways delightedly, doing his best to make that one face that tells people you're having a good time. Tilting his head really seems to help—gravity, baby!

CHAPTER FOUR

Oakland, California

We eat our sandwiches in relative silence, broken only by the constant hum of city noise and the occasional satisfied crunch as one of us takes another bite. For the life of me, I can't remember the last time I've eaten anything so good.

The crab sandwich is a simple Bay Area staple, and its genius was in its subtlety: fresh, lightly seasoned crab piled on top of a lightly toasted slice of San Francisco's famous sourdough bread. The only other accompaniments are a generous slice of tomato, melted jack cheese, and a wedge of lemon to be added at the diner's discretion. No top slice of bread—open-faced is the way to go. The finished product is something that showcases the crab's flavor instead of masking or overwhelming it. The textures work perfectly together: the bread's crunch, the cheese's goo, the crab's easy give.

I had returned to the truck with three to-go crab sandwiches, feeling low but certain that I could find and catch up to Mannie Fuego a second time. After all, how far could a single zombie really get on his own?

As if to confirm my suspicions, I gingerly set the remains of my crab sandwich down in its foam container and unlock my phone. I search hashtags and accounts on Instagram for a bit, but nothing comes up, so I hop back over to Facebook. I scroll through some old stuff, pre-zombification, shaking my head in disappointment, until I see something oddly familiar.

It's a video of me waving frantically from the edge of a pier. It's hard to understand what the me in the video is saying over the blaring Toto song, but I'm clearly pointing and shouting at something near to the man holding the camera. The man starts to narrate.

"This fuckin' douchebag on shore wishes he was here partying with Mannie Fuckin' Fuego, god among men!"

The camera turns shakily to show one of our middle-aged yacht party-goers and Mannie Fuego. The man in question is wearing a captain's hat and a short-sleeved polo shirt. I know I've never met this man, but I hate him.

"Woooo!" the guy says, holding his can of domestic beer aloft. "Say hello to the people, Mannie!"

Mannie tilts his head at the camera and looks for a moment like he might wave. The cameraman turns his lens back on me, zooming in until I'm grainy and amorphous like Sasquatch.

"Later, asshole!" the cameraman finishes.

I do some digging using clues from the Yacht Guy's Facebook account, and to my luck I find that the boat is heading to Oakland.

"Mom," I say, interrupting her crab sandwich reverie. "They're heading to Oakland."

Mom frowns. "You want me to drive us to Oakland now?"

I sigh. "It's either that or you take me all the way back home so I can swap back into the Colt. And may I remind you that town is overrun with zombies? Just drive us over the bridge. We'll get Mannie and be home before you know it."

From the back, I can hear Pop-pop muttering, "Already missed Survivor, what's the hurry now. . ."

Ignoring Pop-pop, I say, "Okay Mom? Can we go?"

Mom gives me a look. "If you say so, but I'm—"

"I know," I finish, "you're staying in the truck." A thought hits me. "But don't you have to pee or something?"

Mom looks suddenly bashful. "I may have already taken care of that."

I don't ask, hoping that maybe Mom worked up the courage to sneak off to the garage bathroom. I know it's a long shot, but the alternative is ... You know what? I don't want to think about it.

Getting through the city and across the Bay Bridge takes way more time than I want it to, which is pretty much par for the course. This trip reminds me why I almost never come here: the traffic is fucking miserable.

The sun has been down for quite a while by the time we get into Oakland. Using the information from the Yacht Captain's Facebook account, I manage to track some of the boat activity and find their landing spot. Mom refuses to go even a half a mile an hour over the speed limit, so by the time we get to the port, the party seems to have been over for quite a while. At least that's what I can glean from the dwindling Facebook posts.

We spend some time (too much time—drive faster, Mom!) cruising around the waterfront until we find the unmistakable wreckage of Mannie Fuego's Party Yacht crashed into the marina. Zombies are milling around on the top deck, giving me hope that Mannie might still be on board. I hop out of the truck, grab my baseball bat, and start to make my way up the pier. A few zombies have managed to climb off of the crashed boat and are making their way toward me, so I start to sing that same obnoxious Toto song to them.

From the back of the truck, Pop-pop shouts, "What are you doing, son?"

Keeping my cadence sing-song, I call back, "I'm siiiiinging to the zoooombies to keeeep them from attacking meeee!"

Pop-pop is quiet for the moment, so I stand there and hum to keep the zombies at bay.

Finally, Pop-pop hollers, "You're gonna kill them when you get close though, right?"

"Um," I say, stopping my singing for a moment. The nearest zombie—who until recently I would have likely described as a middle-aged woman who has clearly had some work done—lunges for me. I scream and shove her, knocking her off the pier. Making absolutely no attempt to swim, she promptly sinks, her bottle-blonde hair the last trace of her as she disappears into the shallow waters. A growl draws my attention, and I whirl and smack the other zombie with my bat. The swing isn't hard at all, and the hit seems to only annoy my attacker, who I recognize as the guy in the captain's hat from that video. Oh how the tables have turned.

"Kill it, Bradley, for fuck's sake!" Pop-pop shouts.

"You can do it, sweetie!" Mom calls, pumping her arms in a gesture of encouragement.

The undead yacht captain keeps advancing on me, jaw slack. Terrified, I swing the bat again, hard as I can. It doesn't even faze the big guy.

"Hey ho, let's go! Hey ho, let's go!"

The music eddies across the water. The yacht captain stops and does his best facsimile of a smile. I look back at the truck, perplexed. Mom is bopping along to the song, cranking it up on the truck's ancient radio. Pop-pop sits in silent disapproval in the truck bed.

"Thanks, Mom!" I say with a wave of my bat before I turn to make my way down the pier. Climbing carefully onto the boat, I push past a few errant zombies as I duck down below, checking every nook and cranny of the ostentatious boat.

Of course, Mannie is nowhere to be found.

Still, he can't have gone far. Quickly as I can, I corral the zombies below deck and throw some tarp over the scattered half-eaten bodies.

When I finally make my way back to the truck, I'm ready to throw in the towel. Mom seems to have been on phone duty while I was gone. Lips pursed, she says, "Looks like he was at a rock show, but it ended at eleven."

"What time is it now?" I ask wearily, leaning against Mom's side of the truck.

"Midnight," Mom says with a frown, handing my phone to me through the window.

"God damn it," I say, ignoring Mom's disapproving scowl as I scroll through the geotagged photos. For what it's worth, Mannie seems to truly be enjoying the Green Day show. At least, that's what I can gather from his very limited range of facial expressions.

"Fuck indeed, Bradley," Pop-pop mutters. Despite his generally conservative nature, Pop-pop loves to swear. He used to get on my case for doing it—maybe because Mom hates it so much—but now that I'm an adult, he's let it go. Mom seems to have given me a pass for the day, too. Maybe she's just gotten tired of snapping at me for my foul language every five minutes.

Pop-pop presses me, "So, what are you going to do now?"

"I..." I scroll around, looking for new information on Mannie. "I don't know. We'll track him down again, we'll stop him!"

"Hmph," Pop-pop says, and I take his meaning. "And what if we don't?"

I frown. In my head, we have no other choice. It's either stop Mannie Fuego or ... I don't know, I guess the zombie apocalypse happens and the end of the world is my fault. I feel a little breathless and light-headed.

Mom speaks up. "If we don't, then we keep going, Dad. We keep going until we find him."

I give Mom a look. "What?"

Mom is staring straight ahead, her hands at ten and two on the steering wheel, as she tells Pop-pop, "This is partly our fault, too, don't you see?"

Pop-pop makes a flabbergasted old man sound. Finally, he manages to say, "I don't see how it can possibly—"

"Bradley was born with The Gift, and we didn't do enough to teach him how to keep it under control," Mom says. "We let him run away from it and repress it, and look where it's gotten us? Did you even know he was using it to freshen up the produce at Bernie's?"

"Your brother doesn't tell me shit, Sarah—"

"That's not my point, Dad," Mom says in that patient but firm way moms seem to all know intuitively. "It's up to all of us to fix this, and if that takes us out to Los Angeles, or Phoenix, or heck, even if we end up in New York City, we're just going to have to deal with it."

Mom finally looks at me, fixing a little smile on her face. "Right, Bradley?"

For the first time all day—heck, maybe for weeks, or even months—I feel reassured. I have purpose, and direction, and the undeniable comfort of my mother's bizarre determination to see this insanity through. I'm sure we'll catch Mannie before he makes his way out of state, and soon this will all have been a very long, strange day.

* * *

Mannie Fuego always wanted to tour the United States with a famous rock band. Of course, in Mannie's wildest, or at least wilder, dreams, he had been the frontman of the rock band and not some D-list celebrity tagalong. Still, as the bus rambles on down the highway, Mannie starts to feel hungry again. He opens his mouth to request a stop at his favorite drive-through hamburger place, but the only thing he can manage to say is "Aaaahhhhhhhh."

One of the band members remarks that Mannie doesn't seem well and hands him a bottle of water. Mannie tries to eat the bottle but decides that the hand that passed him the bottle looks quite a bit tastier.

CHAPTER FIVE

Interstate 15 North, Nevada

Mom is snoring in the seat next to me, slumped over with her face pressed against the window. I absently flip through the radio stations, one hand clutching the wheel at the top. I know that if Mom was awake, she'd scold me for "distracted driving." Nothing but static greets me on every station. I keep fiddling with the dial, asking for something, anything. A voice crackles through the speaker on one of the lower numbered stations.

"Turn around, bright eyes," a falsetto softly wails.

"Fuck, no," I mutter, turning the stations again. Static, static, static, conservative talk radio. I frown and flip back to the 80's station. Total Eclipse of the Heart drags itself on for another mile and fades into U2. I start to wonder if I might have been better off in silence.

We hit a sizable pothole and I instinctively look in the back to check on Pop-pop. I'm not sure why, but I get the impression he's still asleep, too.

We had to stop at a gas station to supply up before leaving Oakland. Because Mom refused to get out of the car, I had to do a more thorough job tying Pop-pop down in the truck bed all by myself, which he berated me for the entire time. Not only was I apparently abysmal at tying stuff down, Pop-pop insisted, but the bungee cords were supposedly cutting off his circulation.

"You don't have any fucking circulation to cut off, Pops. Your insides are all foam and springs," I finally hissed at him. A tall, skinny guy paused mid-swipe as he was cleaning his windows to give me an odd look. I suppose I need to be more careful about arguing with an armchair in public. It wouldn't do to have Pop-pop hauled off by the federal government, or—a much more likely scenario—for me to be committed to a psych ward.

The sun is starting to come up over the horizon, and I stifle a yawn. I have to pee again, likely because I canon-balled three Red Bulls over the course of the evening. Mom should take over driving again soon, though I wonder if she won't wake up with a monster of a fucking crick in her neck.

Everything about this road trip strikes me as insane, but I have to keep pushing panic down and ignoring my common sense.

Over the course of the evening, I kept trying to imagine some scenario that would get me out of this predicament—something that didn't involve me dragging my agoraphobic mother and armchair-bound grandfather farther and farther away from home in what seems to be a never-ending chase. I considered calling the police, maybe dropping an anonymous tip, telling them Mannie Fuego is going on a murderous rampage. But I talked myself out of it. Hypothetically, when and if the cops caught up to Mannie, they would quickly figure out that something was off about him, wouldn't they? And then they'd be searching for the source, the thing that turned him into a zombie. And where was the last place Mannie had been seen acting at least like a semi-normal human being?

No, cops were too risky. And, after cops, I had no ideas for solving this that didn't involve me. I keep considering turning the truck around and dropping Mom and Pop-pop off at home, but in my heart of hearts, I know that doing so will only allow Mannie to get farther away from me. And the longer Mannie is allowed to run wild, the more likely it becomes that authorities will notice something is off about Mannie, and my predicament starts anew.

"I knowww this muuuuch is true," someone croons from the radio. I angrily jab at the power button, preferring the silence.

Through the cab's back window, Pop-pop gets my attention. "Hey, Brad?" Maybe I was wrong, and the pothole woke him up after all.

"Yeah, Pop-pop?"

"About those zombies back on the pier. . ."

Oh boy, here we go.

"What about them?"

"Ya shoulda killed 'em."

I'm glad Pop-pop can't see the face I'm making. He'd say I was being disrespectful. With a sigh, I say, "Yeah, I know."

"Gotta practice swingin' that bat, huh?"

My frown deepens. "What if I don't want to kill them?"

"Oh, for fuck's sake, don't be going all soft on me like that."

"I'm—" I blow a frustrated breath out through my nose and gather my thoughts. "I'm not being soft. I just think it's wrong to kill those people."

"Zombies, Brad. They stopped being people the second Mannie bit them."

"Well, we're just going to have to agree to disagree on this one."

Pop-pop harrumphs and says, "Well, son, even if you spare every last zombie Mannie makes, you're still going to have to kill the man himself. And if you can't do it with that bat of yours—and it looks like you can't—we're gonna have to get you a gun."

Louder than I mean to, I snap, "For fuck's sake, Pop-pop, I get it!"

Mom startles awake, half-choking on a snore she had been working on. To my great relief, Pop-pop finally shuts the hell up.

"Oooh," Mom moans, rubbing her neck. "That smarts." Blinking the sleep out of her eyes, Mom looks around at the flat nothing around us and asks, "Are we close?"

"I think so," I say, squinting around. "Last sign I saw said thirty more miles." I look over at her. "You okay? Need something to eat?"

Mom nods. "I haven't had anything since those onion chips last night."

Her breath is a testament to this.

"You sure you want to stop, though?" Mom asks.

I nod. "We need food. I need a rest. If the band really does end up in Vegas, at least they'll stop when they get there and give us some time to catch up."

"Good plan then," Mom says.

"So what do you think about breakfast? I saw a sign for a Denny's about a mile back. Maybe I'll order us some waffles or—"

"Oh!" Mom perks up. "No no, Bradley, I have a much better idea!"

"What's that?" I ask, forcing myself to keep my eyes on the road to avoid kick-starting her anxiety.

"There's a Tasty Train in Vegas!"

I feel my jaw clench reflexively.

Mom frowns. "What's wrong?"

"I don't know," I say, trying my best to sound casual. "You don't think it's weird, eating at one of Mannie's restaurants while we're chasing him down on a mission to kill him? I feel like that's weird."

Mom's eyes get wide.

"What?" I ask, "Okay, I'm sorry, we can go to Tasty Train—"

"Kill?" Mom asks, her voice quavering. Pop-pop remains conspicuously silent.

"Um," I say, hoping the non-word will save me and hold my place in the conversation while I try to catch my brain up with what's going on. I had thought that killing Mannie was implied when we left the house, and that Mom was well aware of what we were up to. Licking my lips, I say, "Yeah mom, I mean. . ." I heave a sigh. "We have to kill him, Mom. There's no other way to stop him. Pop-pop said so. . ."

"Dad said STOP Emmanuel. We have to STOP him. STOP doesn't mean KILL."

She's shaking now, and I wish I hadn't just pissed Pop-pop off so he would help me out. Alone, trapped behind the wheel of the car, I'm afraid to even make eye contact with her. I know I need to tread lightly, so I say, "Well, um. Maybe we can find a way to stop him that doesn't involve killing him? I don't know, it's a long shot, but—"

"Well, you have to TRY, Bradley." She's shaking, and her breaths are starting to come in short gasps. "You have The Gift, maybe you can use it to magic him back. You have to try at least, right? You can try to—"

"Sure, Mom," I say quickly, hoping to defuse her before she has a full-blown panic attack. "I can definitely try. Maybe Pop-pop has some tricks I can try."

"Good," Mom says, blowing the word out like a cloud of smoke. "Good," she says again, sitting back in her seat and taking a few deep breaths.

We drive on in relative silence until we spot Green Day's bus in an embankment on the side of the road half a mile outside of Vegas. At this point, I'm less than surprised to find that Mannie has fled the premises. Inside the bus, I'm grateful to find that the band has only been turned and not killed. I leave them there—after snapping a selfie with them for posterity that is. I mean, when am I ever going to get a chance to meet Green Day again, zombies or otherwise?—and lock them back inside the bus. As I walk back to the truck, Mike Dirnt is pressing his face against the glass and mouthing zombie nonsense at me.

"Bye Mike!" I say, waving. I love Green Day.

Back in the truck, Mom asks, "Well? Did you find Emmanuel?"

"No," I sigh, "But we may as well keep on our way and stop by the strip. Tasty Train awaits, and I know how bad you want to try Mannie's signature truffle fries."

"Ooooh, I do!" Mom says with a little clap, revving the ancient engine and turning back onto the highway.

* * *

Mannie Fuego often fantasized about being involved in one of Penn and Teller's famous magic shows, and today is his lucky day.

Teller seems to be deep in concentration as he does something with a magical floating ball, and Penn is off to the side explaining what the two are about to do to Mannie as the riveted audience watches silently. It's all pretty technical and hard to follow, so Mannie just stands there enjoying the mystical music and the shiny red ball. It's all so much fun!

In fact, everything about Las Vegas makes Mannie's cold insides warm up a little bit. After all, he had opened his first ... something in Vegas. What was it again? Something about the Tasty Train. Maybe he had operated a train depot. That made sense.

Anyway, Mannie had been drawn to Vegas years ago like a moth to a flame. Everything about it—from the lights, to the music, and definitely the way Vegas embraced day drinking—fed Mannie's soul. He made his way to the city of sin as often as he could and, even in his altered state, knew his way to the strip like the back of his hand. He lost track of how long he wandered around, enjoying the noise and bustle of the strip, before he rode the wave of foot traffic directly into a matinee magic show.

As usual, Mannie was recognized in the crowd and invited to be part of the magic. Mannie tried to make that face that told people he was delighted as he had ambled up to the stage. Now, he stands center-stage, bathed in the supernova-hot glow of stage lights, waiting for whatever super rad magic spell Penn and Teller are going to cast on him.

But when Penn finally finishes his speech and takes Mannie by the shoulders to guide him to his mark, another feeling washes over him. Penn is a big man, after all, and Mannie hasn't eaten for a while...

CHAPTER SIX

Las Vegas, Nevada

I always wanted to go to Vegas. It was a check on a long list of iconic cities I had dreamed of visiting. At first, I considered trying to go for my twenty-first birthday. But that date came and went, and I ended up spending my twenty-first birthday alone with a piece of cake I bought for myself at the grocery store and a single tall-boy of local beer.

Most of my high school friends turned twenty-one in college and posted pictures of themselves on Facebook holding up colorful shots and cocktails and getting progressively more drunk. They posted about their usual college watering holes as they rolled on from twenty-one to twenty-two. Soon enough, those same friends were posting pictures of themselves toasting champagne or drinking celebratory bloody marys in their caps and gowns as they graduated and moved on with their lives.

Now that I'm twenty-five, some of my older friends are getting married. Instagram posts of wild nights out are being replaced with pictures of engagement rings and puppies. Others are establishing really good careers. Even the ones who had done neither of those things are traveling, and some of those friends have invited me on weekend trips to Vegas or backpacking trips around Thailand. But I always stayed put, cooking fries with Bernie and watching Survivor every week with Mom and Pop-pop. Some of my friends still say hello when they come home to visit for Thanksgiving or Christmas. Others have inevitably drifted away as their lives and careers took off. I never begrudged them that.

Standing on the Las Vegas Strip, admiring the riot of flashing lights—garish and beautiful all at once—I feel a strange pang of regret.

This isn't the first time I've had to consider every wrong turn I ever took in life, starting with that infamous day in bio. Why hadn't I forced myself to go back to school and just dropped biology? Or maybe I could have really fought to skip the dissection lab—I could've gone vegan or even vegetarian and really argued that cutting up dead animals was fundamentally against my world view. (I mean, in reality, it kind of is.) I should have fought harder, tried to get through.

"Ifs and buts," I say to myself, shaking myself out of my reverie and turning toward Mannie's famous Vegas strip restaurant.

Mannie Fuego's Tasty Train is every bit as ridiculous and kitschy as I expect it to be. Mannie Fuego built an empire of restaurants based on his signature catchphrase, "Hop aboard the tasty train!" And, because Mannie Fuego is in insufferable douchebag, every Tasty Train restaurant is meticulously themed out to look like the inside of a train car, and servers are forced to degrade themselves with awful train puns at every turn.

Sitting alone in a booth, I admire the strange mix of people who have been drawn into the Tasty Train this morning. There's a group of blue-haired old ladies thoroughly enjoying their time on the tasty train as they dig into their Engineer's Eggs Benedict and Platform Pancakes. Ranged around a wide table in the middle of the main dining area are the hungover remains of a bachelorette party, some of the girls still in their stilettos and tiny dresses. Others are in sweatpants with their party makeup looking a bit worse for wear. The bachelorette, still in a white dress and a sash that says "BRIDE 2 BE," looks like she's a heartbeat away from puking into her Wayfare Waffles.

In a far corner is a family, possibly on a cross-country road trip? The son is involved with his handheld game (I lost track after the PlayStation Vita, to be honest) and the elder daughter looks bored to death as she scans something on her phone. The midwestern-looking mother and father are chattering to each other, clearly pleased with the pun-laden restaurant they've dragged their tortured-looking children into. In spite of myself, I feel an odd pang of jealousy.

"Welcome to Tasty Train," a bleary-eyed waiter says as he bumps up against my table, "where everything on the menu is just the ticket. Would you like to start off with an appetizer to chew-chew-chew on? Or perhaps something to drink?"

Apparently they couldn't think of any clever puns for the beverage ask.

"Uh, yeah," I say, scanning the beverage menu. "Can I have a coke?"

"Sure, one Coal-Car-Cola coming right up. Would you like that to be a big chug, medium chug, or little chug?"

I stand corrected.

"Um, medium?"

"Perfect," the waiter says. "I'll have that out on the express line."

I know it's early to be drinking soda, but I hate coffee. I apologize to my teeth as I scan the menu for something I won't be too embarrassed to ask for out loud.

The waiter returns, and I order Mom's truffle fries (Tasty Train's Famous Tonnage Truffle Fries! Served all Day!), a stack of the Wayfare Waffles for Pop-Pop, the Bulk Breakfast Special for myself, and the Flimsies French Toast for everyone to split. I consider ordering the Hogger Heaven too, which is literally just a plate of bacon and sausage, but think better of it.

"And can I get this to go?" I add. "I'm in a bit of a hurry."

"Sure thing, and do you want any of that Double the Hill?"

I make a face. "I'm sorry, I don't...train puns," I say, putting my sleepy face in my hands in defeat.

Clearly used to patrons being frustrated with the overuse of niche train vocabulary, the waiter asks, "Do you want us to split all of those orders into separate boxes?"

"Yes," I say. I can't imagine what it might look like if everything was put into one big container. Leave it to Mannie Fuego to create a restaurant that can actually do that kind of thing.

I open my phone to see if Mannie Fuego has popped up here in town and start scrolling. I see a lot of posts about Mannie Fuego from the Green Day concert last night, which makes me feel a pang of guilt for the zombified East Bay punkers stuck in their tour bus. Hopefully I can set this all straight when I get to Mannie.

Mannie.

Someone has snapped a selfie with him on the strip in front of the Bellagio, and the time stamp is from just fifteen minutes ago.

After what feels like an eternity, the waiter is back with our food and a bill.

"Your order and the bill of lading," the waiter says, gently placing two bags with foam food containers onto the table. I glance at the bill and throw enough cash down to cover the total plus a fairly generous tip. As I practically fly past the hungover bachelorette party, the waiter yells after me, "I hope your Tasty Train experience made the grade!"

I'm crunching on some of Mom's truffle fries as I make my way down the strip. It just made more sense to leave Mom safely locked in the truck with Pop-pop while I wander around looking for Mannie. I personally don't get what the big deal is about the truffle fries, but Mom gushes over them. She claims the texture is better, and the touch of garlic is just right. I was more excited about the French toast, myself. Nothing beats a perfect piece of French toast, and as much as I'm growing to hate Mannie Fuego, I have to hand it to him for running a tight ship ... or, in his case, a tight train, I suppose.

Even at this hour, everyone is so drunk it's hard to tell if any of them have been turned. Alright, maybe some of them are just doing that slow-shuffle tourist walk that I hate. Still, by the time I make it to the Bellagio, Mannie has moved on.

I wander the strip for hours, looking for any sign of Mannie: zombies, gore, general mayhem. Frustrated, I check my phone again. After what feels like the fiftieth Minions meme that day, I finally spot Mannie Fuego again.

There he is, standing on stage with Penn and Teller. According to the gushy Facebook post, Mannie was in the audience and got recognized by Teller, then pulled onstage to demonstrate a magic trick. The poster then goes on to admit that she didn't understand the latter half of the trick, when Mannie bit Penn Jillette's hand off and proceeded backstage, but that's the mystery of magic!

I Google the address and start running.

* * *

Mannie Fuego always imagined that when he retired, he would do one of those bus tours around the United States. So when he finds himself shuffling onto a bus full of senior citizens on the strip, Mannie figures he must have lost track of time. A lot of track of a lot of time. Mannie considers the possibility that he is senile now, and this is just what it feels like to be old.

Still, Mannie very much enjoys the bus ride and the kind-voiced woman who calls everyone's attention to various points of interest on the PA system as they slowly drive out of Las Vegas.

CHAPTER SEVEN

Still in Las Vegas and Generally Hating My Life

I find Penn and Teller backstage. Teller is eating what little is left of poor old Penn.

As I consider what to do with Teller, a few undead stagehands wander into sight, and suddenly I'm surrounded. They lurch toward me, eyes manic and hungry, and I'm panicking. Out of nowhere, music starts to blare over the PA system:

"Ladies up in here tonight! No fightin'," Wyclef Jean intones.

I look everywhere, trying to figure out who or what queued the song.

The zombies are soothed by the bright horns and Wyclef's continued insistence that the ladies not fight. As the song continues into Shakira's signature brand of Latin fusion pop, I take a moment to survey the area in search of a good place to trap the swaying zombies. I catch sight of a dressing room and cautiously make my way toward it, picking up a fallen mic stand and holding it like a kendo stick to push some of the docile zombies out of the way as I head toward the door.

"Oooooh I'm on tonight, you know my hips don't lie and I'm starting to feel it's right," I mumble along with Shakira as I usher the zombies into the cramped dressing room.

Locking the door, I leave a note in case anyone happens back here before I'm able to take out Mannie:

'PLEASE BE WARNED: ZOMBIES IN HERE. DO NOT OPEN.'

I make my way back out to the empty stage, stopping and frowning at a small pool of blood marring the polished wood. Without warning, the stage is flooded with bright lights, and a voice comes over the PA. "Just who are you, anyway?"

I think if I were any more startled, I might piss my pants. Thankfully,

I manage to keep it together. Shielding my eyes from the lights, I see a shadowy figure up in the theater's control booth.

Bolstering my voice over the music, I say, "Uh, hey up there. I'm Bradley."

The music abruptly stops and the voice from the booth asks, "Who?"

"Bradley," I repeat loudly as I can. "Or Brad. Only my mom calls me Bradley. Can you come down here? It'd be easier to talk."

"Are those ... things still down there?"

"No, they're locked in Penn's dressing room."

"And you're sure it's safe?"

"Yes," I say, already getting tired of making reassurances. I need to get going and find out where Mannie is off to now.

Within moments, a diminutive woman with pixie-cut bleach blonde hair is walking up the theater's center aisle. She's dressed the way I've come to expect theater people to dress: in varying shades of black. The light hits her nose ring as she tilts her head to cast a furtive glance over her shoulder, clearly worried that I haven't adequately dealt with the zombies backstage.

"So," she says as she draws near, "Bradley. What brings you here? It can't be your love of expertly crafted stage magic. . . ?"

"No," I say, charmed by her speech mannerisms already. I should've come to Vegas years ago. "I know this sounds crazy, but I'm looking for Mannie Fuego. Last I heard he was here, onstage?"

"Yeah," the girl confirms. "He was here all right. He ate one of Penn's fingers right on stage. The fucking rubes in the audience thought it was a goddamn magic trick. I faked a technical failure and got everyone out of here." Instead of heading to the stairs, she places her palms on the stage and hops up in one smooth movement.

"Good thinking," I say, and I really mean it. I love clever people.

"Thanks," she says with a little smile. I feel my heart skip a beat. She offers me a hand up on stage, which I gladly take. It's only after I'm standing near her again that I start to wonder if I smell bad.

Gesturing at the empty seats, she goes on to explain, "After the public cleared out, I went backstage to try and figure out what was going on, but by then it was too late. I'm the only person who works here who hasn't turned into one of those monsters." She frowns. "I know this sounds selfish, but I don't know what I'm going to do with Penn and Teller dead. I guess I'll have to look for another show to do tech for. Then again, with my boss also dead, I'm not going to get any good recommendations. This fucking sucks."

In spite of myself, I laugh. Seeing her narrow her eyes at me, I hurry to apologize. "I'm sorry ... um?" I realize I never got her name.

"Penelope," she says, picking up on my tone.

"Penelope," I confirm. "I just didn't expect your first concern to be work. I mean … truth be told, you're the first survivor I've met."

"Survivor? What, are we in some kind of zombie apocalypse?" she teases, looking around the room as though it might fall down around us.

"Not yet, no. I've been running around stopping it happening so far, but if I don't catch up to Mannie—"

"Oh my god, you're serious." Her jade green eyes are wide with— what, surprise? Disbelief?

My lips form a flat line. "Penelope, I wish I wasn't."

She thinks for a moment, then a wry smile breaks across her face. "I see."

"You see? You're being remarkably cool about all of this, you know?" Something hits me then. "Wait, are you a necromancer too?"

Penelope's smile gets bigger. "No, my family is mostly healers." And the way she says it, I know she's not fucking around.

"Oh my god," I breathe, wishing I could take her to coffee, then dinner, then talk with her under the stars all night. "I... You..."

"Here." She takes my hand and wipes a thumb over a huge spreading bruise on my forearm. The purple-black washes out of my skin like wet ink under her warm touch. As I watch, she explains, "So … you made all these zombies happen? I imagine it was an accident."

"Yes," I take a breath, starting to say something, then stopping. I imagine I look like a trout. Feeling awful, my hand creeps to the back of my neck as I tell her, "I might still be able to fix this, but I have to track Mannie Fuego down first. Did you see where he went?"

She nods. "I was trying to stop him, but he ended up following a group of old ladies onto one of those Tour America buses. He's quite the wanderer."

"Tell me about it," I say with a frown. "I'm sorry this happened to you, but I'm glad you're not hurt."

"Small miracles, I suppose," she sighs. "So … why Mannie Fuego?"

"He was the first one I turned," I say with a feeble shrug. Her expression begs an explanation, so I add, "It was an accident, I swear. And since I turned him, I'm the only one who can stop him, I guess. And if I do, everything should go back to normal. Including Penn and Teller."

Lips twisting, she says, "Well, good luck to you. I think you should be able to look up the bus route and figure out where Mannie is off to now. Those Tour America buses have pretty static routes."

I look around the empty stage and catch sight of Teller's foot from the wings. Guilt washes over me again. "I'm really sorry about all this," I say lamely. "Do you maybe want to come with me? You'd be safer than staying here."

She shakes her head. "I've got people to look after. And three big dogs, to boot. I'd just slow you down."

"Right, I shouldn't assume everyone's a big loser like me who can just leave everything behind." I sigh. "I should be getting back to my family. Just, if you see any more zombies, they seem to be calmed by music. Play the music, pen them up, try not to kill them?"

"I won't. Healer's honor." She winks, putting a tiny hand out to shake mine. "Well, I wish you the best of luck on your journey. I guess I'll hold off on job hunting for the moment?"

"Do," I insist. "I'm going to fix this."

Penelope laughs. "If you say you're going to fix this one more time, I swear I'm going to lose it. Besides,"—she sighs, looking around the stage—"If I'm being totally honest? I always felt a little weird doing a fake magic show, given my own capabilities."

"God, I wish I could hear all about this—why did I have to meet someone like you out in this mess?"

"Fate?" she asks impishly. "But hey, let me add you on Facebook. That way, we can talk more AND I can look you up and come kick your ass in person if you fail."

I can't stop my face from breaking into a stupid grin.

It's my turn to drive again, and Mom is snoring in the passenger seat. I keep playing my conversation with Penelope over in my head, wondering how many other people have been fucked over by my mistake.

It didn't take a ton of digging to figure out where Mannie's Tour America bus is heading, and I program each planned stop into my phone's GPS. The next major stop on Mannie's U.S. Zombie tour is the Grand Canyon, but I imagine I might catch up with the tour group at a rest stop or something. Instead, we're always just a hair too late, following Mannie's trail of cannibalistic destruction like a macabre trail of breadcrumbs. Everywhere we go, I take a moment to corral the zombies and cover up the destruction. A part of me wants to turn on the national news to see what the authorities are saying about what's happening, but I refrain. I know it'll just freak me out.

My determination reminds me of people who play the lottery. I'm certain that every new destination will be the one where I finally catch up to him. I guess at this point, I have to keep telling myself that or succumb to the hopelessness that keeps threatening to swallow me whole.

"Hey," Pop-pop stage whispers through the window. "Your mom asleep?"

"Was the snoring not a big enough clue for you?" I snicker.

"Hey now, no need to be a snot about it, Bradley," Pop-pop huffs.

"Sorry, Pops." I cast a glance at him over my shoulder. "Mom's out cold. What's going on?"

"I heard you two talking this morning, about not killing Mannie Fuego."

I perk up. "Is it possible I won't have to kill him? Did you remember a spell?"

"Don't be stupid, Bradley, of course you'll have to kill him!"

"Oh," I say, reaching for my Red Bull and taking a long pull from the can. It tastes like what might happen if you mix gummy worms with battery acid and soda water, but it gives me a much-needed jolt. "So, if you didn't remember a spell or anything, then why are you—"

"Pretend, Bradley."

"What?" I narrow my eyes at the road in lieu of being able to make faces at my grandfather.

Pops sighs. "When you finally kill that sonofabitch, you kill him dead. But if your mom is anywhere nearby, I want you to pretend to cast an incantation."

Resettling my hands on the wheel, I say, "Pop-pop, no disrespect, but how do I pretend to cast a spell? Do I just mumble some hocus pocus nonsense or—"

"No Bradley, your mother will know." The way Pops says it, I'm expecting him to say duh, just to rub it in. "The words are simple, but they won't do anything: IMORIUM NYROS."

"Imorium nyros," I repeat.

"That's the ticket, son. I know it'll break her heart if you kill Mannie, but at least this way you've tried ... or pretended to try."

We pass under another streetlight, briefly painting the car in splashes of yellow-orange, illuminating my mom's sleeping face. Just as quickly, the truck's cab is submerged in quiet shadows. The thought of lying to my mother, of causing her any grief, makes me sick to my stomach. I consider saying as much to Pop-pop, but I know he'll scoff and tell me I'm being soft again.

* * *

Mannie Fuego always meant to tour the Grand Canyon and do one of those donkey rides into the gorge.

He decided that retirement wasn't all that bad after all; his new friends kept the oldies playing on the bus all afternoon, which Mannie very much liked. Plus, they did all of the talking, saving Mannie from the embarrassment of his newfound lack of speech. A few of his new friends seem to be afflicted with the same thing: they don't say much, and their faces are slack and expressionless. Mannie is starting to feel that perhaps he has finally found a place where he belongs.

But, as his donkey slowly makes its way down the trail, Mannie starts to wonder when the group is going to stop for food. It's been a while since he's had a proper meal.

C H A P T E R   E I G H T

Grand Canyon National Park, Arizona

If I'm being honest, being at the Grand Canyon kills me. I wish that somehow, Mannie Fuego would have diverted his course away from this place. I don't have any idea how he sat quietly on that bus full of old people without attempting to eat a single one. Maybe Penn and Teller filled him up. Maybe the people running the Old People Tour Company doped him up on whatever it is they give the elderly so they don't throw a fit in those assisted living homes.

Hell, maybe it was the old people smell.

Either way, he somehow made his way here. He must have. The old people don't really post anything on social media. Most of them don't even have smart phones and wouldn't know what it was if you told them. Okay, that's ageist. I'm sure they do. I just don't talk to many elders other than my armchair-bound grandfather, and he's the exception to just about every rule there ever was. It wouldn't be fair to paint his entire generation with his special and peculiar brush.

No, my clue for finding Mannie Fuego is a solitary family picture shared by a man named Robert Dvorkis. The family is carefully crowded into the frame, all riding donkeys down to the bottom of the Grand Canyon. Robert is in the foreground, riding a particularly bored-looking donkey and looking every bit the embarrassing tourist dad: bucket hat, khaki cargo shorts, and wire-rimmed glasses complete with clip-on sunglasses. Presumably, Mrs. Dvorkis (or, I don't know, I suppose she could have kept her maiden name?) is the woman grinning toothily behind him, leaning precariously to one side as her donkey bears her weight with the patience of a true-born champion. The Dvorkis children are close behind, the elder son looking a bit bored and put out while the younger son grins and throws up a peace sign. It's a charming family photo, one that fills me with a sickening sense of envy, but that's not why I'm stuck on it. Just behind the Dvorkis family is our friend Mannie Fuego sitting astride his own donkey and looking—as much as a dead person can, I suppose—like he's having a great time.

That was the last update I saw from Mannie. It was a few hours ago, which—if I can trust my Google-Fu—means he's heading down to the bottom of the canyon to camp. Even if he wanders away from the camp tonight, he'll be stuck on foot, so I've got good chances of catching him.

Looking around at the scenery, I feel really cheated by photographs. No flat image can ever do justice to seeing the canyon in person. Weirdly, I'm hit with the impulse to snap a picture. Silly me.

We were supposed to come visit the Grand Canyon when I was nine years old. Dad planned everything down to the littlest detail, including a donkey ride down to the bottom, followed by camping out under the stars. But the day we were supposed to leave, Mom pulled the plug. At the time, Dad told me she was sick, but I've been able to put the pieces together over the years.

Her agoraphobia started small. I remember her having a couple of panic attacks when I was really young. (Again, something I've managed to deduce as an adult. When I was a kid, I just thought she got really sick at the drop of a hat.) She'd get red-faced and start to shake and sweat. I remember being about ten when she had one in the grocery store checkout line. We were about to pay for a cart full of groceries, and I was really excited because Mom agreed to buy that cookie dough that comes in a tube. She'd been complaining that she wasn't feeling well through the whole shopping trip, but something in her just snapped while we were unloading our food. Someone called an ambulance.

Anyway, after that first canceled Grand Canyon trip, Dad promised we'd go the next year. But, as you can guess, the next year came and went, and Mom "got sick" again. The year after that, Dad was dead.

So, basically, fuck the Grand Canyon and the donkey it rode in on.

Mom's in the passenger seat so she can take in the sights, and she's been ooing and ahhing for the better part of an hour. This is perhaps because we are literally driving to the bottom.

Allow me to explain.

It took some figuring out, but there happens to be a dirt track that goes to the bottom of the canyon. It's on tribal land, and—understandably—local tribes don't want tourists to just go wandering onto their land and getting stuck when they make the foolhardy and altogether ill-advised choice to drive down one of their more rugged roads. However, Pop-pop knows a guy (not sure how, and I was told not to ask) and managed to connect me with someone willing to look the other way.

I'm glad for the help, but it'll be a miracle if I get through this without wrecking our fucking tires.

In spite of the clear duress our car is experiencing, Mom is having a ball. Watching her enjoy the views, seeing her be purely joyful for the first time in a long time over anything that isn't television ... it's nice.

Pop-pop, on the other hand, is throwing a grand mal hissy fit.

He's yelling at me about everything he can possibly think of: the truck's suspension, his bad back, the tires, and generally just how much of a fuck-up I am. At first, I'm able to tune him out and focus on driving, but I'm hungry and exhausted, tired of being the only one in this little trio who can actually do anything. At least Mom drives sometimes, but Pop-pop?

I try to steer us around a particularly nasty pothole (is it considered a pothole if the road isn't paved?), but it catches the outside of the driver's side front tire and sends all of us flying (at least as much as anyone can in seatbelts). The suspension squeals, I nearly smack my head on the truck's roof, and Mom is moved to utter a fervent, "Oh dear!"

From the back, Pop-pop wails, "God damnit, Bradley, are you TRYING to drive like shit?"

"Fuck, that is IT, Pops!" I yell, pulling off to the side of the road, as if stopping right there in the middle would inconvenience anyone.

"What, what's the problem Bradley?" Mom asks as I try to click the giant red plastic seatbelt button. The damn thing sticks every time, so you have to really jam your thumb into the fucking button, which ends up with your thumb getting bitten by old shitty metal half the time. Though, considering my luck, I think I end up with a scraped thumb more than half the time. Of course, the button sticks now, and a particularly tender piece of thumb flesh is trapped and chewed up before I can even get out of the fucking car.

By the time I'm facing Pop-pop down, I'm furious—and I mean heart pounding, literally feeling those white-hot flashes of rage, seeing them in real time like lightning fury. I know I look ridiculous, mean-mugging a fucking armchair, squaring up like I might just punch it. Where would I even punch this thing? Never mind, I'm talking about punching my grandfather. I clearly have issues.

Pop-pop seems to be watching me, assessing what it is I might do next. "Well, son?" he asks. "You gonna hit me?"

"No, Pops, I'm not going to fucking hit you."

"Well," he says, and the way he says it, I know he'd be resettling himself, or perhaps stretching out his neck if he were standing. "You shouldn't square up in front of another man like that unless you're planning on really doing something. Otherwise you might end up—"

"I don't fucking care about your dipshit old man advice right now!"

If an armchair can look taken aback, that is exactly what Pop-pop is doing right now.

I continue, "You've been bitching and moaning all the way down this fucking road. Meanwhile, you've done exactly zero things to help me find Mannie. Got that? Exactly zero."

I know how ridiculous I sound. I'm spinning out on my own rage, drunk on the feeling of just letting it out of my chest. I'm tired and hurt and angry and I need to make him feel every bit as bad as I do. No, I need to make him feel worse.

"In fact, you haven't lifted a finger since you conveniently magicked your old ass into that fucking arm chair, so next time you decide to criticize me—or Mom, for that matter—just remember all the bullshit you've put us through thanks to your dumbass fucking mistake."

"What—" Pop-pop blusters. "What did I put you through, I just—"

"We had to get rid of the cat because he kept clawing your upholstery! We have to bring you every single meal of the day because—somehow, inex-fucking-plicably—you still need to eat despite the fact that you inhabit an inanimate object that has neither a mouth nor an asshole. What the fuck are you, just a black hole of food consumption? Do you shit dust bunnies?! I need to know!"

I'm out of rage, and now I'm just sputtering every bit of nonsense rattling around in my brain, every minor grievance, every stupid thing I've refrained from saying out loud in better mindsets.

Pop-pop clears his throat. "Well I … didn't know you felt that way, Brad. I always kind of thought you and your mom enjoyed having me around still, since your dad—"

"I don't want to fucking talk about Dad right now," I seethe, though my pulse is finally slowing down.

"That's alright, son," Pop-pop says, and his tone is far too kind considering what I just threw at him. "Why don't we get to the bottom of the canyon, see if we can't catch up to Mannie. You and I can talk about this later."

No matter how old I get, Pop-pop will always have the ability to pull rank and be the better adult in the room. Feeling more than a little ashamed, I climb back into the cab. Mom is making a big show of looking like she hadn't been listening to and watching our entire confrontation with her undivided attention. I pull the seatbelt back across my chest and click it into the buckle, watching the heinous little red button snap into place with what I can only call a self-satisfied little click.

That's right, I'm so fucking angry I'm personifying seatbelts now.

I start the engine and we trundle on down the road, practically choking on the silence we've all tacitly insisted on for all these years.

I want to say I'm lost in the beauty at the bottom of the Grand Canyon, but I'm not. I'm fucking over the goddamn Grand Canyon, and I have been since about five minutes after we got here. Every bit the elder brother in the Dvorkis family portrait, I hate the Grand Canyon, and I want to go home.

The Colorado River is wide and casts the sunlight back at me as I stare blankly across and down the gorge. It is at this moment that I realize the fundamental flaw in my plan: the Grand Canyon is fucking massive. The idea that I could have come down here and found Mannie Fuego on foot is completely laughable. Pop-pop had every right to yell at me earlier. I *am* a fuckup. My plans are short-sighted, and I'm always trying to find the easy way out of things. If I'd have hopped on one of those damn burros and ridden down the side of the canyon, maybe I would've caught up to Mannie, but I hated the idea of leaving Mom and Pop-pop alone for so long. Of course, I didn't say as much to either of them at the time because—as we discussed earlier—the people in my family don't say things until they're well past pissed off and words are no longer a useful means of conveying anything but our mutual frustration with each other.

It is, of course, at this very moment that I spot something on the river that makes me question my belief in anything but the universe's enduring love of a good joke.

* * *

Mannie Fuego had never been much of an outdoors type, but he always imagined it would be fun to take one of those whitewater rafting river trips. You know, just so long as he didn't have to actually do anything.

Having eventually grown bored with his time spent in retirement, Mannie wanders away from the campground he's sharing with his elderly friends and finds himself being invited to join this rafting trip. Sadly, his arms don't work so well, and the raft people make him wear a helmet and life vest, which really doesn't go with Mannie's look. He tries to tell the rafting instructor as much, but, as usual, words fail him.

So, as Mannie glides down the Colorado's easy currents, guided by his raft-mates and surrounded by a flotilla of admirers, he decides he very much enjoys the outdoors. And, as a lone blue-haired kid waves and screams at him from shore, Mannie is comforted by the fact that that no matter where he goes, he will always have his fans.

C H A P T E R   N I N E

Somewhere Between Arizona and New Mexico

I'm watching myself scream on the dusty shore of the Colorado river.

"Hey Mannie, dude, looks like you've got a fan," someone narrates from off screen.

It's GoPro footage. Of course the river rafting guide had one strapped to his helmet, like some kind of alien apparatus for the douchiest race of extraterrestrials ever to come to Earth. I'm not totally against people using GoPros—people have done some pretty cool things using them—but the average human has no business strapping a camera to their head to record their every move. In the case of our whitewater rafting friend, the footage is shaky, the narration useless at best and obnoxious, stereotypical bro drawl at worst. The camera pans around the river, then shoots back to me, crystal clear this time but looking just as crazy as I appeared in the yacht video from before. If I'm not careful, I'll turn into a meme. I'm screaming for Mannie Fuego, and at one point I start to wade into the river.

The problem, of course, is that I can't swim.

I watch myself realize that I can't make myself learn how to swim— at twenty-five, no less—with Mannie Fuego slowly getting away. It would have been foolish to try. I mean, even if I succeeded, I'd be murdering Mannie Fuego in front of all these poor people, because apparently none of them can tell that the fucking idiot has been dead for two days. I suppose that's really less of a condemnation of their intelligence than it is of Mannie's, though.

I'm wet and shivering as Mom drives us back to civilization and food. We're all starving—though Pop-pop would have words with me if I used that particular word out loud.

"You've never starved a day in your life, Bradley," he would admonish, and he's right.

But fuck it. It's my story, and we're starving. There, Pop-pop. I said it.

I feel like the world's biggest idiot for losing Mannie for the second time, foiled again because Mannie somehow found his way onto a boat. Or maybe it was a raft? Either way, I try to work out the most logical conclusion to Mannie's river trip in my head.

First off, there's no way Mannie's making it all the way to the Gulf of California on that raft. It would take an extraordinary set of circumstances, including him eating or otherwise killing all the tourists that are on the raft with him, which could potentially get him free of the rest of the tour group. Even then, Mannie would have to stay put on said raft and not get beached or … rescued? Would that be the right term to use? Or by that point, would he be apprehended because he killed people? I can't imagine people would continue to assume everything was fine with Mannie if he killed innocent tourists in front of even more innocent tourists. Then again, I've made the mistake of underestimating people's capacity to excuse Mannie's behavior before, so here we are.

I'd about kill for a shower and a bed to sleep in, but I'd feel like a total asshole for leaving Mom to sleep in the truck with Pop-pop while I crashed out in a real bed. Besides, I have to keep following Mannie down the river now, I guess—at least, as closely as I can in the truck. I realize now how much better off I'd be sending Mom home with Pop-pop and renting a car to finish this out on my own, but I don't know what might happen to the fragile stability Mom is holding on to if I were to suddenly up and leave.

I've had a lot of time to think over the past couple of days, and I have to assume that Mom is okay in the truck because it's familiar, like a little moving piece of home. Maybe in her brain that's enough separation from the chaos of the rest of the world to make this journey possible. Maybe having Pop-pop close by, as he has been for years, is just enough of a facsimile of our living room to allow her to maintain the veneer of calm she's been holding on to. Whatever it is, I'm afraid to tamper with the ingredients, especially when I can only guess the recipe. No, best to stay close. I was the one who dragged her out of the house in the first place. Of course, she wouldn't have been safe at home. Home is overrun with my Wagyu Zombies. Half the town came to Bernie's that day, and the other half … well, they're bitten or eaten by now.

Mom pats my hand, a move that reminds me of when she used to drive me around as a kid. She did it whenever she sensed I was thinking too much, wrapping myself up in a blanket of my own anxieties. She called it chewing on thoughts.

"You chewing on your thoughts, Bradley?" she asks now.

"Yeah," I say, not looking at her but grateful for the small comfort of her words. Can you be nostalgic for a question?

"Well, we'll get you fed. Maybe we can find a place for you to take a shower and get some dry clothes. Would you like that?"

If her tone is placating, I don't mind. I need her to be the adult for a moment.

I haven't spoken to Pop-pop since I blew up at him. He hasn't spoken to me either, so at this point I think it's safe to assume that we aren't speaking to each other. I can't remember the last time I really fought with him like this. The discomfort of that thought adds to the pile of worries I'm currently trying to sort through. While I'm ashamed of the things I said to him, there's a part of me that's holding on to resentment and isn't ready to let go. Maybe I want to win the argument, or maybe I just don't know what to say. Probably, it's everything. I'm tired and starving and scared and angry and hurt, and everything is congealing into a joyless stew in the pit of my stomach.

"Bradley?" Mom asks. By her tone, I can tell she's about to ask me something serious.

I'm afraid to respond, but it's not as though I can pretend I didn't hear her. "Yeah, Mom?"

"Bradley, we need to talk about Dad."

Shit.

"Mom, we don't need to talk about Dad. Maybe we can talk about him when we get home? When this is all over?"

I'm not looking at her, but I can tell Mom is frowning. "I've had a lot of time to think these past couple of days, and I realized that after he died, we all just … I don't want to say we didn't grieve, because we did, but we also made a big point of moving on. There was a lot we never got to settle, you know?"

I feel queasy. "What's there to say, really? I mean, of course I miss Dad, and losing him was devastating, but"—I swallow hard—"what's done is done, right? He's dead, and we can't change it."

I feel like maybe I'm being excessively deliberate with my word choice, because there's something there I don't want Mom to ask me. I don't want her to even think it, to even hint that she could be thinking it.

"Bradley, I know you probably felt a lot of pressure to find your gift. To 'save' your father. But…" She sighs. "I need you to know that he never would have wanted things that way. I suppose that's why your grandfather refused to spell him into anything."

I'm staring down at my hands, letting the weight of Mom's words fall over me. I keep still, afraid to disturb any of them, terrified to touch them for fear of having to deconstruct them and apply them to my life. Because what she's saying, they aren't just words. They have the potential to recolor my late adolescence.

See, I lied to you earlier when I implied that the discovery of my gift was terrifying. Don't get me wrong, bringing a dead cat back to life was definitely a shock to the system, not something I recommend to anyone with a fragile temperament. But what really upset me that day was that my gift had come to me so late, far too late to make any sort of difference in whether or not I got to spend any more time with my father.

The day he died, I ran out of the house and didn't stop until I got to the creek. I was eleven years old, which, according to Pop-pop, was too old to show any prowess with "The Gift." No, if I hadn't shown any inkling toward black magic by that age, I never would. Still, when I got to the creek, I hunted relentlessly for something that had sent me running away from the creek a few days earlier.

I didn't know how the faun died; all I knew was that, when I found it and realized it wasn't asleep, something inside me shrunk away, curling up like a cat being held over water. Looking at that dead young thing, miserable grief overcame my senses and I ran home, crying furiously. Dad comforted me that night. I know now that, to some fathers, an eleven-year-old boy shouldn't cry over dead animals, but Dad got me in a way no other human has ever been able to. Mom always said we were two of a kind, kindred spirits. I always liked when she said that.

Still, the day Dad died, I sought that deer out. I needed to find it, to prove something. Maybe, I remember thinking, the extraordinary circumstances would draw the magic out of me, and I would be able to perform the dark miracles my grandfather boasted about when he had too many beers.

The faun was where I left it, strangely untouched by roving scavengers. It was as though it was being protected by its own innocence, too small and perfect to be reduced to blood and bones. I remember approaching the faun with intense trepidation, certain that I would somehow pollute it with my magic and it would spring to life like a macabre toy. But the deer did nothing no matter how close I got or what words—nonsensical or otherwise—I muttered at it. I don't remember how long I stayed down at the creek, prodding and shouting at that corpse, but it was dark when I got home.

I always assumed it was my fault we didn't get to spend more time with Dad. I also assumed that Pop-pop didn't deign to bring Dad back to life because the two of them had never really gotten along, because Dad didn't approve of necromancy.

It takes me a long time to realize I'm crying. I'm a blue-haired twenty-five year old and I'm bawling as my mom drives me to get dinner.

Mom doesn't look over, but I'm sure she hears me.

"Bradley, there's a lot about death that's hard. For necromancers, I think it can be even harder. But at the end of the day, all our magic can do is blur the line between living and dead. We can't create immortality or delay what the universe has planned. I never had The Gift, but I saw the way your grandfather moved through life. How devastated he was when my mother died."

Mom never talks about Grandma. She died a year after I was born, so although I technically did meet her, I of course have no recollection of the meeting or any of the time I spent with her. What I do know, or what I've been able to gather through observation, is that Mom still hurts. Twenty-four years later, the absence of her mother still chafes her. I imagine the grief like a broken bone, something you manage to heal from, mostly. But when the weather turns rainy, the old pain springs back to life, and you ache from something you keep assuming is long healed. It's how I feel about Dad. Mom seems more put together with her grief. She at least had her mother through her childhood.

But what I always wondered about all of this was why anyone we loved had to die when we have this bizarre gift to reanimate the deceased.

Then again, is Mannie Fuego really living? Or is he just a hungry corpse going on one last adventure before the real end finds him?

I'm shaking, my throat aches, and the tears are coming on in torrents. I can't remember the last time I cried. I think it might have been the night Dad died, when I failed to save that faun. Now, though, I'm starting to wonder if I've had it wrong the whole time. The faun died long before I wandered into its resting place, and yet I've been carrying the burden of not being able to change the unchangeable all this time.

The truck stops. Mom pulls me close, and I bury my wet face on her shoulder.

* * *

Mannie Fuego always meant to go skydiving, at least once in his life.

There was something about jumping out of a plane; Mannie was sure the act was proof positive that he was a brave motherfucker. Mannie always dreamed of doing an episode of *Mannie Fuego's Guide to Good Eats* where he went skydiving, but the producers never bought it. "What does skydiving have to do with food, Mannie?" they would always ask.

Nothing. Skydiving had nothing to do with food, but it was awesome, and at the end of the day, weren't they all just trying to make good television? If they needed a food angle, Mannie could eat a hot dog or something in the air! Television producers could be so damn short-sighted.

Mannie is glad for the change of pace. The river trip got boring fast, fans or no. Still, it was difficult to recall the events that brought him to the skydiving place. He remembered his river friends very quickly paddling him to shore after he snacked on one of them. Luckily, Mannie had fans wherever he went, and he quickly found some new friends as he went in search of a good meal. They invited him on the skydiving trip, and Mannie did his best to look excited. He opened his mouth wide and hoped he looked psyched.

The plane ride is quite nice; the plane guys keep playing power ballads as they climb high into the sky. The only real disappointment is that—yet again—Mannie is being forced to put a helmet on over his sweet 'do. Admittedly, Mannie does feel better about wearing a helmet when they give him one with cool flames painted on it. Still, as everyone starts jumping out of the plane, Mannie starts to wonder when lunch is going to be. Now, as he gently floats back down to Earth with another dude strapped to his back, Mannie wonders if he might get away with nibbling on a finger or two. . .

C HAPTER T EN

Texas

We had just crossed the border into Texas when Mom demanded we stop and get some chicken fried steak at a place where Mannie had done an episode of *Mannie Fuego's Guide to Good Eats*. She did the same thing several times when we were in New Mexico, insisting on trying everything from posole to Frito pie.

Of course, in Arizona we got some of the best burritos we've ever had—and that's coming from a kid who grew up in California. There's something about a good burrito, whatever your fillings of choice are. I like to mix it up. I'll take a vegetarian burrito with the works, extra guac, wet or dry. I like a carnitas burrito every now and again. If I'm feeling spendy, I'll throw down extra for a good steak burrito though, especially if it's carne asada with a killer marinade. It's hard to do a burrito wrong, but Arizona seems to have the burrito game on lock.

Now firmly in the state of Texas, I apologize to my heart as I dig in to an order of chicken fried steak. It's excellent: perfectly breaded and fried cube steak topped with gravy. I've had plenty of chicken fried steak in my day, but it's been greasy or chewy. This, though ... This melts in your mouth. The crunch is perfect, and the breading is seasoned with precision. Of course, the steak comes with a generous wedge of honey corn bread and a side of mixed vegetables I'm sure most people ignore. I eat everything, as does Pop-pop. Mom's appetite is a little daintier, so I help polish off whatever she can't get through. The sacrifices I make.

We've been following Mannie's path of destruction west from the county fair for a few days, and he's been incredibly busy on his journey.

We caught up with Mannie after he made land and ran into a group of bros who, for reasons I'll never understand, invited Mannie to go skydiving with them. Really, it's a miracle Mannie didn't crash the plane. Instead, he ate most of his tandem diving instructor before they hit the ground. Not sure how Mannie accomplished that in the harness, but that's Mannie for ya.

From there, Mannie seemed to have hitchhiked with a group of college kids on a road trip into New Mexico. We found the wreckage of their car on the side of the road, along with some newly made Mannie-zombies, but no sign of Mannie. After that, Mannie ended up at a county fair pie eating contest. Of course, Mannie didn't appear very interested in the pies in the picture someone posted from the event. I can only assume Mannie ate his way through a record number of pie-eaters that day—we never saw the aftermath, because he popped up in a selfie with a truck driver heading into Texas before we made it to the fair. I had to hand it to Mannie; people seemed to love him wherever he went.

For our part, Mom, Pop-pop, and I were starting to enjoy ourselves. I mended fences with Pop-pop somewhere near the Arizona-New Mexico border.

"Bradley, you don't need to apologize," Pop-pop had said after my long-winded apology. I kind of hate when people say that, because of course I needed to apologize. That's just other people's way of trying to be big and humble when they've received an apology. Still, the way Pop-pop said it wasn't as aggravating as it could have been. I understood what he meant: Pop-pop was saying it in a "we were both being jackasses" kind of way.

I know this because he went on to say, "We were both being jackasses. I know you've got a lot on your mind, what with chasing down Mannie Fuego and whatnot, and I know I'm not much use here in this chair. Guess sometimes I let my mouth run away with me, you know?"

I was still feeling sore, but I let myself smile. "I know, Pop-pop. It runs in the family."

Now we're due west, following the truck driver's route into Dallas because, luckily for me, the truck driver had captioned his photo thusly:

"Look who I found on I20 today? Rollin' into Dallas to party my ass off with this fuckin' superhero!"

He then proceeded to add twenty hashtags, including #WhereTheHottiesAt. I will not feel sad for this man if Mannie eats him, and I don't care if that makes me a bad person.

Mannie has gone dark for a few hours, which I can only assume means he has managed to refrain from eating or otherwise maiming anyone for a little while. Small miracles.

I've been thinking about Dad a lot. Part of me feels like an old wound is finally starting to close up, and as I distance myself from the guilt and misery, I can hold up my memories of my dad and look at them without feeling sick or nervous.

Mom used to work in the afternoons, so Dad used to be the one who picked me up after school. It's weird to think that this was only routine for a few years of my life. The hours we spent together are etched very precisely into my brain. Then again, I've heard that memories aren't the cleanly recorded eyeball-videos we like to think they are, but stories we tell ourselves over and over again. That's why people's recollections of big moments get warped with time, why your grandfather catching a mediocre bass will eventually turn into his epic battle with an eighty-pound lake monster.

Still, I like to think that I've done a good job of preserving my memories of the afternoons I spent with Dad, like a very careful and diligent museum worker or one of those comic book collectors who wears gloves when they take issues out of their hermetically sealed plastic sleeves. I approach these memories with a sort of reverence, because—cliche as it may sound—they're all I have.

The routine was like clockwork. Dad would roll up to the school's driveway and pop the door open, always grinning wide.

"Hey, buddy! Need a ride?"

He would say it with one eyebrow cocked, as though expecting that I could say, "Nah, Dad, I'm cool. Thanks though."

My dad had this effortless cool about him that was in no way limited to the 'I'm a cool dad' vibe that my friends' dads never seemed to be able to shake. Now that I'm older, I realize this is likely because my dad was one of those rare humans who is totally at ease with himself and his role in the world. He knew what he liked and didn't bother much with what he didn't like. If you put on a song he didn't care for, he wasn't going to fuss over it. He wouldn't even tell you he disliked it unless you bothered to ask.

There was really only one thing Dad went out of his way to show his disapproval for, and that was Pop-pop's gift.

It wasn't that Dad was religious and disapproved of Pop-pop's work with Satan worshipers. If anything, I think Pop-pop's mercenary attitude was something Dad found amusing, though he would never have admitted it. No, what Dad disliked was the disruption of what he saw as the natural order of the world. He saw Pop-pop's gift as something that tampered with that order. Pop-pop's magic had the potential to rip apart the carefully structured world Dad was sure existed around him.

Ever since that day in bio, I've often wondered what Dad might think if he knew I had "The Gift." Would he be disgusted to know that his own son had the potential to rip holes in the fabric of reality? Or—had he still been alive—would the discovery of my gift be the thing that finally brought him and Pop-pop together? I know that, if Dad had been around that day I went running home from school in my rubber apron, he would have made me face biology. He wouldn't have let me drop out. I wouldn't have wanted to disappoint him.

When I was little, we would go straight home every day except Friday. Fridays were our weekly holiday and, in celebration of having made it to another weekend, we went out for ice cream, regardless of the weather. Dad was of the opinion that ice cream was a fine treat whether it was ten degrees or a hundred and ten.

When we got home, Dad would crack a beer and I would sit down at the kitchen table with my homework. He sat at the table with me and sipped at his beer, flipping through the paper or cruising on his laptop, and he'd always give me his full attention the moment I spoke up to ask for help. Dad was smart. There wasn't a single subject where he would admit, as many adults do, "Oh, I never did well in that class." He seemed to enjoy studying every subject, which I found strange, because I developed a broad range of feelings about the various subjects in school by second grade. Dad was patient, though. He'd listen to my tirades about math and, once he was satisfied I said my piece, would help me through the problem. No speeches about why I should like math or how it would help me, just calm acceptance that it wasn't my thing and the help I needed to learn it anyway.

After homework, we'd get started making dinner. Really, he did most of the work and I would fetch things. As I got older, I helped chop and grate. Dad loved to cook, and I loved to watch him cook, loved the way the kitchen smelled as he brought meals together.

Mom usually got home just as dinner was finishing up, and she'd have a kiss for each of "her boys." Dinner spelled the end of our afternoons together, the point in the day when the family became a single unit again. After dinner, we might watch something together or fracture to pursue our own leisures. But the afternoons were our singular constant thing, a routine Dad refused to break regardless of whatever got in the way. Sickness, appointments, car issues; nothing stopped him. Even if he knew I was going to a friend's house after school—which I rarely did—Dad would still drive up to the school and check in with me, ask if I might need that ride after all.

This is why I flew into such a panic when, on a fairly nondescript

Tuesday afternoon in fifth grade, my father failed to show up after school and offer me that ride home.

I waited at first, calm with the knowledge there had been the odd time Dad was late for one reason or another. It was rare, but it did happen. When five minutes late turned into fifteen, then twenty-five, I was jumping out of my skin. Sometimes, you just know something has gone wrong.

I ended up walking home, and by walking I, of course, mean running as fast as I possibly could, which isn't easy with a backpack weighing you down. Well, that and we lived three miles from the elementary school. I couldn't run the whole way nonstop. I was never athletic to begin with anyhow. I can still remember the sharp pain in my legs, the way my lungs felt like they couldn't take in enough air. My fingers started to tingle, and black spots erupted in my vision. I would walk just long enough to get my wind back, then push myself to keep running. People looked at me like I was crazy, and I hoped to death that they were right, that I was forcing myself to run an impromptu 5k this afternoon for nothing. I'd round the corner for our street and find my dad under the hood of the car, smoke billowing all around him. He would hear me pounding the pavement and turn, give me that smile he always wore when he picked me up, but this time his eyebrows would be just a little turned up in the middle in an expression of remorse, because he felt bad for making me worry.

Dad would get the car fixed and drive us out for ice cream, even though it was only a Tuesday. From there, the night would resume its regularly scheduled programming. Homework. Dinner. TV. Mom would tuck me in and Dad would come in to sing the goodnight song. Everything would keep going, on and on in that perfect pattern.

But, like I said: sometimes, you just know something has gone wrong.

When I finally rounded the corner, I saw the car was in the driveway, just sitting there. I felt like kicking it and almost did as I rushed by. The door was unlocked, which wasn't unusual when Dad was home working. He did freelance website design from "his office," which was really just our garage. Mom always complained about not being able to park in the garage, but Dad made good money, and it was convenient for all of us that he was there when I got home from school, that his schedule was flexible.

The moment I had the door open, I remember calling out for him, my voice thready and weak from the running. When he didn't answer, I panicked. I pushed my vocal chords to make the sound louder, shouting "Dad! Dad! Dad!" and checking every room as I ran through the house, shoes and backpack still on, body slick with sweat.

I found him in his office, slumped over his desk. He was cold to the touch, and when I shook him, he didn't respond. I ran to the phone, dialing 9-1-1...

This is why I don't think about him. Because that day inevitably pops back up. Because as much as I love picking up the good memories, this will always be the last time I saw him alive. I don't want to, but this is inevitably how I remember him.

"Sweetie?" Mom says tentatively, "We're in Dallas."

I'm surprised to realize that I've dozed off. I had been trying to force myself to keep my mind off Dad by thinking of nothing, counting cars, keeping track of license plates. Now, I'm rubbing the sleep from my eyes and looking around.

"Fuck," I say, forgetting in my sleepiness how much Mom hates profanity. "Some traffic, huh?"

Mom's mouth twists into a frown. "Yeah, they've been reporting it on the radio. Ten-car pile-up, and it all started with a big rig."

I've already got my phone out, and I'm canvassing social media for any sign of Mannie. He's already made it into Dallas proper. People are posing with him at every conceivable landmark. The last post has him outside of Dr. Pepper Ballpark, home of the local minor league team: the Frisco Rough Riders. It was posted less than a minute ago.

* * *

Mannie Fuego always dreamed of throwing out the first pitch at a major league baseball game. Unfortunately for Mannie, this was just the minor leagues, and his pitching arm was acting up. Mannie remembered being able to pitch a pretty wicked splitter back in his high school sports days. Granted, it had been a minute since then, but Mannie still thought he should be able to give the ball a good throw.

The crowd was cheering, reminding Mannie that his adoring fans were expecting something. He found himself wishing he could explain that he hadn't been feeling like himself lately, but when he opened his mouth, his tongue slid uselessly over his teeth. It was all Mannie could do to keep his tongue from lolling all the way down to his chin.

As the crowd's adulate cheering slowly turns to boos, Mannie finds himself thinking that the Frisco Rough Riders don't deserve to be treated that way. Hoisting the ball over his head, Mannie decides that he is going to throw the greatest pitch anyone has ever seen.

CHAPTER ELEVEN

Arkansas

I'm starting to feel the effects of eating famous Southern cooking for every meal, so today I'm eating fruit and yogurt for breakfast. Mom is at the wheel, as she is for most of the daylight hours.

Since we passed into Arkansas, I've enjoyed delicacies like possum pie. (No actual possums are harmed in the making of possum pie; it's a dessert with a name that makes you think southerners eat possums.) Possum pie is a pretty basic dessert—layers of whipped cream and chocolate cream on top of a butter crust. I regret not grabbing a second helping, because the dessert was everything. It was comforting and creamy, a little tangy, but perfect in its simplicity.

Mom insisted we stop for fried pickles at a place Mannie Fuego featured, and of course, despite the fact that fried pickles sound disgusting, I ended up really enjoying them. I like pickles, so I'm not sure why I thought fried pickles would be gross. We've also eaten okra, chocolate gravy, and some of the sweetest watermelon any of us have ever tasted. Of course, the entire southern part of the United States is known for its barbecue, and we've had plenty of that since we crossed the border into Texas too. Pop-pop's complaining about his blood pressure, which Mom and I have generally been ignoring because ... well, because he's an armchair. I think maybe he routinely complains out of habit, and maybe he forgets that he isn't in a flesh and bone body anymore.

Last we saw Mannie online, he was riding into Arkansas with the Frisco Rough Riders. This after he failed spectacularly at throwing out the game's first pitch. Watching it back online, I found myself wondering if Mannie might lose his arm. He wound up like a baseball player in an old Looney Tunes cartoon, which is more vigorous movement than I have seen out of him since he turned undead. Granted, his wind was incredibly slow. Maybe Mannie thought he was winding fast—it's hard to tell what he's thinking, if he's thinking at all. After his ridiculous long wind, Mannie finally released the ball, which promptly dropped to the ground at his feet.

The crowd went from booing to stunned silence. Finally, the announcer cut the tension.

"Well, folks, looks like Mannie's been hitting the hooch a little early today! Let's have a round of applause for our friend from the Food Network!"

Mannie looked into the camera at that, his expression shifting ever so slightly. To me, it looked like he wanted to say something about hopping on the tasty train, but I haven't seen or heard Mannie say anything since I turned him, which is in keeping with my assumptions about zombies.

"Well, of course he can't talk," Pop-pop says when I bring this up to him. "He's dead."

We're sitting in the back of the truck together, snacking on more fried pickles while Mom naps in the cab.

"Sure Pops, but, I mean, he's still walking and seems to have some gross motor function left. Why is it safe to assume that he can't talk?"

Pop-pop sighs. "Because he's undead. You used your gift to bring him back—whether you knew it or not—but you granted him little more than the ability to be an empty, shambling corpse. He's a bag of bones and flesh, somewhere between here and the Great Beyond."

"So there's nothing left of the old Mannie in there?" I ask, feeling a little bad.

"There could be," Pop-pop says. "Nobody knows for sure, seeing as how zombies are terrible conversationalists." Pop-pop thinks for a minute. I'm not sure how I can tell he's considering what to say next, but something about the set of his cushions looks thoughtful. "I've seen zombies show glimmers of their old selves. Familiar people, places, maybe songs can awaken things in them, stir something from their human life. It's hard to say for sure what causes those small glimmers of memory, but I have seen it."

My stomach knots. "You made zombies?"

If Pop-pop had a face, I know he'd be frowning. "Bradley, we have The Gift."

"That doesn't answer my question," I accuse. "In fact, I don't think I know anything that you did for the Satanists."

"That, Bradley, is because I made a point of not telling you about my work. You've always been sensitive."

"Well, sensitive or no, enlighten me. What did you do?"

I'd thought that Pop-pop and I were good after we mended fences a few days ago. We've been good, chummy even. But under every conversation and new exotic food, there's been a thread of tension, small but insistent. Neither of us seems to have forgotten about our argument, and since Mom and I had our chat, something has been bubbling under the surface. I'm fighting a long-suppressed anger, something I had all but buried years ago, and I think Pop-pop is at the crux.

"Bradley, the work I did with the Satanists was low-key at best. I never actually raised the dead for them, or did any of the other nefarious things you seem to think I've done."

"Then what—"

"I attended some black masses, but mostly I was the black wizard in attendance at their weekend getaways. I would put my 'dark blessing' on things, which was really just mumbling nonsense over altars and other items. Satanists are generally pretty good people, Bradley. They want the same things everybody else wants."

"Oh?" I ask, cocking an eyebrow. "And what's that?"

"They want to go about their lives, enjoy time with the ones they love, go to work or school, and spend time doing the things that make them happy. Satanists, Christians, atheists, necromancers, magical, or mundane—most people just want to live a simple life with the people they love. I didn't do anything to disrupt that with my gift.

"Necromancy is a complicated power to possess, and I know now that I didn't do enough to prepare you for the powers you have. I guess … I guess when you showed signs of finally having The Gift, you were so upset I didn't want to make that worse. Your mother and I both coddled you like that. That's our own failing."

"So, what's the point of even having these powers, then? If all we can do is raise the dead and disrupt the natural order of things? Why do it at all?"

If Pop-pop had shoulders, I know he'd shrug. "You may as well ask why water's wet. It's not for us to know why we were born with The Gift."

"But you've seen zombies before? How?"

"Bradley, you think you're the first guy to accidentally start the zombie apocalypse? This is the fifth one I will have put down in my time. If anything, sometimes I think necromancers exist to keep giving people the impression that the veil between the living and the dead really exists. We strengthen the idea. Most people are more comfortable with the idea that dead is dead, and that's that."

I've lost my nerve, and I don't feel that same nervous energy I had before. As much as I want to confront him about Dad, I can't.

"You know, Bradley," Pop-pop changes the subject, "you should probably take some practice shots with that gun before we run into Mannie again. You don't want to miss him once you've got him in your sights."

We had taken advantage of Texas's lax red state gun laws and picked up a small handgun before crossing the border into Arkansas. Right now, the gun lives in the truck's glove box. Before putting it in there, I made sure the safety was on, several times. I have bullets, too, but I can't bring myself to try to load the thing.

I very much doubt that I can shoot Mannie Fuego, even if I manage to get within point blank range of him. I can't even look at the gun I bought, let alone shoot it. Pop-pop is right in that regard, I suppose.

Pop-pop sees the look on my face and says, "You can just set up some cans, shoot them like kids do with BB guns. I can teach ya. Shoulda taught ya a long time ago, really."

"Dad wouldn't have liked that," I say, surprised to have brought it up at all.

Pop-pop is quiet for a moment, contemplative. "No," he finally sighs, "I don't suppose he would have. He was a good man, your father. Didn't always agree with him, but he was a good man nonetheless."

"Still," I say, "I'm an adult. I make my own choices. I think it's time for you to teach me how to shoot, don't you?"

Something in the set of Pop-pop's cushions tells me he's smiling.

* * *

Mannie Fuego always thought it would be neat to be part of a high-speed police chase.

Mannie was beginning to get used to finding himself in strange situations. Something was off with his memory, and he was still entertaining the idea that he might be going senile as a result of old age. Mannie supposed that getting old and senile could result in forgetting the past thirty years or so.

So, when Mannie ends up in the passenger seat of a speeding car, he and his companion bathed in the candy-colored lights of half a dozen squad cars, Mannie can't admit to being surprised. If anything, Mannie is just bored, and a little hungry. He considers asking his new friend to pull over and stop for some McDonald's or something, but when he opens his mouth, whatever he might be saying is drowned out by the wailing sirens.

Looking over at his friend, Mannie tries to recall what brought them together. Had it been his new friend's love of driving? Mannie is too famished to think straight.

He decides maybe it would be alright to sample his new friend, just take a nibble. It had been a long time since Mannie rode the Tasty Train. Unfortunately, his new friend isn't steady behind the wheel, and as they veer off the highway and barrel toward the ravine, Mannie smiles. Or, he contorts his face in what passes as a smile for him these days, which is really more tilting his head and hoping his mouth falls open in an expression that resembles joy. This is more like it! This is the police chase he always wanted, like the end of that one movie.

CHAPTER TWELVE

Western Tennessee

I'm standing in a broad, flat, quiet field. It's quieter here than any space I've ever seen in California and, subsequently, in my life. That's why I feel so bad squeezing off round after round of bullets into every bottle and can the state of Tennessee has to offer.

Okay, that's a bit of an overstatement, but I feel like I've been standing here doing this forever.

Bullets are expensive, but I've managed to save quite a bit living at home, so I don't mind spending a few hundred dollars to stock up on magazines. It's crucial that I learn to aim and shoot without hesitating or missing. When I find Mannie, I doubt I'll have much of a chance. I still can't gun him down in front of witnesses, which complicates things infinitely. Why no one can see that Mannie is not—in fact—touring the United States in a state of perpetual and sometimes endearing drunkenness, I'll never understand.

At the moment, I'm actually more concerned that Mannie is going to be arrested. Last I saw news of him, he was "hostage to" the most wanted felon in the tri-state area, speeding away from the cops into western Tennessee. The felon was apprehended after crashing his car, which I'm SURE Mannie caused. Still, I'm on pins and needles. I mean, if Mannie eats someone in front of the cops, it's over, right? Drunk people don't eat other humans. Other, very alive, humans. Then again, there was that guy who was high on bath salts a few years ago. People had been whispering that it was the dawn of the zombie apocalypse then, and that the government was in the midst of an elaborate cover-up.

Oh, shit.

"What's wrong, Bradley?" Pop-pop asks.

Oh, right. Pop-pop and I are alone together in this field. Mom insisted she needed to go see something on her own, so she took the truck and left. I was surprised that she helped me off-load him from the back. Of course, she wouldn't let her body break contact with the truck's body, but I was still shocked when she opened her door and slid out, albeit slowly. I'm even more shocked that she drove away without us, like it was nothing. The truck is like a low budget, agoraphobic popemobile or something. She feels invincible in it, safe and secure. It's like a psychological exoskeleton. Maybe when this is all over, I can convince her to start going back to therapy. Hell, I'd actually be fine with her walking around town in a big metal suit like Iron Man if it got her out of the house and actually living again.

Now that I'm thinking about it, I think I know why Mom took off this afternoon and left us in this field, actually.

Today is Mom's birthday. And, before you condemn me for being a bad son, it's not that I forgot and she drove off in a huff to be alone with her feelings. Mom hates her birthday, and not in a way that a lot of people like to hate their birthdays as they get older, when they start celebrating the first, second, and third anniversary of their thirty-fourth birthday and so forth. Mom actually used to love her birthday. In our house, it was a tier-1 holiday, like Thanksgiving and Christmas, and it garnered as much attention and time. Unfortunately, a lot of that energy used to come from my dad.

The more time and distance I get from home, the more I find myself thinking about him. It's as if a spell has been lifted, and all of these memories are trickling back into my brain. Back home, I had settled into a routine. Everything was so rote, and I realize now that I left myself very little time to be idle and think. I know, you're probably thinking, "This guy was a fry cook at his uncle's hamburger restaurant in a go-nowhere town in Northern California with very little education and zero ambition. How on earth could he stay so busy?"

My idle moments were consumed with reading, video games, podcasts, movies, and television. Back home, I always kept a steady flood of words around me, letting them rush into my brain and shut out anything else that might be trying to elbow in and get some attention. It worked. At work, I listened to podcasts pretty much nonstop. At home, I read a lot. I like to think the reading helped me make up for what I lacked in formal education. It at least allows me to speak like I'm not a high school dropout. Thank you, books. I also played games, enjoying the ones that didn't let my mind wander and forced me to stay present, solve puzzles, anything. Even then, I usually had music going at the same time if I could, just to keep my thoughts quiet.

But now, I'm surrounded by deafening silence. Music on the radio makes me crazy, so I more often than not shut it off and let everything that I've avoided thinking about sweep over me. I can feel a perceptible shift in my inner narrative, the way I'm feeling and reacting to the world around me. That's why, now, I'm trying to figure out how to make Mom's birthday not suck, even while we're out in the middle of the United States chasing down an undead Food Network star. I guess the best thing to get her for her birthday would be to not kill Mannie Fuego, which I still haven't been able to break to her. I'm hoping I can just lie, tell her I tried to cast a spell but couldn't. When I bought the gun, I told her it was Plan B. Pop-pop seemed to be glowering at me disapprovingly through the back window but stayed silent.

"What's the matter, son?" Pop-pop asks. I realize I've been aiming at an empty beer can for a while but not shooting.

"Mom's birthday is today," I say.

"Yeah," Pop-pop says. "Hard for me to do much about it, though. Your dad always made a big fuss about Sarah's birthday."

Mom's birthday used to start with Dad making a big breakfast: waffles, French toast, fried eggs, omelets. No matter what he made, there was always a giant plate of bacon to accompany it. One year, he taught himself how to make crepes, and you'd best believe they were fucking amazing. He'd wake Mom up with breakfast in bed, but she'd insist on eating breakfast with the family. It would be the three of us sitting around the table, stuffing our faces before nine. We'd eat so much, we usually skipped lunch.

Pop-pop would drop by for dinner, usually around five. He'd bring Mom a gift, always something simple like a plant (Mom loved plants) or a gift card. The advent of gift cards had been a real boon to Pop-pop. It took all of the guesswork out of his gift buying. If he knew which stores you liked, bingo. If he didn't, he'd usually just get you an Amazon card and let you have at it.

In the afternoons, between the insane breakfast and the extravagant dinner with Pops, the three of us would head out to the city. Mom used to really love visiting San Francisco. She had always been anxious around people, but something about being out with me and Dad kept her steady. We'd go to the botanical gardens, or the Academy of Sciences, or the pier. We'd spend an afternoon walking around and working off that breakfast Dad made. This was where the big breakfast came in handy, of course, because we usually didn't need to stop what we were doing to eat.

On the way back, we might grab milkshakes or smoothies to snack on during the drive. At home, we'd do presents as soon as Pop-pop and Uncle Bernie came over—if Uncle Bernie joined us. He used the restaurant to get out of a lot of family functions, which I can't say I really blame him for. Then, we'd all go out to the local Italian restaurant. It was Mom's favorite, and mine if I'm being honest. They made this burrata and prosciutto plate that I could never pass over. Dad would always poke gentle fun at me for eating an appetizer for dinner, which didn't stop him from insisting he get a few bites, of course.

Dad always waited until dessert to give Mom her gift. Looking back on it, I think maybe he liked the moment because it would all feel so perfect. Everyone would be full of good food and heavy carbs, drunk on good wine and cocktails or—in my case—cheese. We'd be halfway through the warm, sticky sweet desserts Dad would insist on us ordering, at ease in the restaurant's soft lights, our faces illuminated by the low flickering of the cursory table candle. That's when Dad would produce a package, usually small, and hand it over to my mother with a sort of reverence I assume people used to use only for kings and queens. Every year, the gift was perfect. It was precisely what my mother wanted that year, every year, which was impressive because my mother rarely made admissions out loud to really wanting anything. But Dad had a habit of watching people and listening really closely. He could always parse out what it was you really wanted, even if you yourself hadn't quite recognized it. Mom would lament that her favorite necklace had broken or make an off-hand comment about how much she had enjoyed learning to knit when her mother was still alive. It was all Dad needed.

That was how her birthday went for eleven years, and I have to presume that it had been that way for the handful of years my parents were married before I came along as well. Dad made Mom the center of the universe that day, which isn't to say that it was too terribly different on other days. Dad and Mom always had this connection that—even as a young child—I could tell was special. And not just in that "Mommy and Daddy really love each other" kind of way. There was something about it that I didn't see in my friends' parents. I know it sounds cliche, but I mean it when I say those two completed each other.

I guess it should come as no surprise to you that Mom's agoraphobia came on much stronger after Dad died. Her refusal to leave the house was something that happened slowly and all at once. She began to miss things here and there, until suddenly she just didn't go anywhere. And by that time, I had grown accustomed to this. It started to feel like the days when we would go to San Francisco were part of another life, or something I had dreamed.

I can't help but wonder where Mom is now, what she's up to.

I tried to make Mom's birthdays special after Dad died. I made breakfast, and when she refused to go out, we would stay in and watch Mom's favorite movies. Instead of eating dinner at the Italian place, Pop-pop would order it to go and bring it all home in a series of take out boxes. It was a shadow of what her birthday had once been, and while Mom would never say so, I could tell that she missed Dad more on her birthday. It got to the point where she asked us not to do anything and, after a few very awkward years, we finally acquiesced to her wishes. Lately, her birthday was just another day on the calendar, nothing special, and definitely nothing worth acknowledging with even a cursory "happy birthday, Mom." The most I could get away with was very quietly bringing home a cake, and even that was a risk.

Taking aim, I suck in a breath and pull the trigger. The beer can I've been aiming at goes flying off its perch with a satisfying metallic ping.

"That's my boy, you're getting it," Pop-pop encourages. I feel like he's been going out of his way to be supportive, maybe as a way to make up for pushing me to deal with guns at all. Then again, I mean, he might be right about this gun thing. This could be my best bet. I haven't managed to kill a single zombie during this whole mess, anyway, and as much as I like to think I could just bash someone's skull in ... Never mind, I don't like to think that at all. At least shooting someone is somewhat impersonal.

I hear a car coming along the dusty goat track that passes for a road out here. Mom's coming back.

* * *

Mannie Fuego always thought he would get the key to the city. Any city, really.

As Mannie tried to take stock of his life—which was admittedly difficult to do when he was having so much trouble remembering just about anything—it was becoming clear that Mannie was finally getting to live the life he had always meant to live. No more boring trips to Nowhereseville, USA to feature someone's family recipe for pork and beans for Old Mannie! Now, he would be recognized as the national hero Mannie was always meant to become.

Mannie couldn't remember how he helped the police, but they sure were grateful for whatever it was he had done. It had been a narrow miss the other day, with his friend in the car and the cliff they nearly drove right off of. The police congratulated Mannie on his quick thinking—"What had made him think to bite the perp?" they kept asking.

Mannie tried to explain to the police that he had been very hungry, and biting was something that came naturally to him these days, but he couldn't think of the right way to say it.

Now, as he stands on the steps to city hall and accepts a key that Mannie very much doubts actually opens all of the doors in the city, Mannie wonders where his newly charmed life might take him next. He hopes that wherever it is, there would be a buffet.

C H A P T E R   T H I R T E E N

Nashville, Tennessee

I'm exhausted.

We've been following Mannie at a cautious distance since he received the key to the city in Nashville. I watched the entire thing via Facebook livestream, waiting for the moment Mannie would snap and eat someone. It never happened, and I can only assume that the fanfare and music kept Mannie from taking a bite out of anyone.

Mannie hasn't gone far since the ceremony, but he's been surrounded by people the entire time. Somehow, Mannie is being hailed as a hero who managed to stop a high-speed police chase and rescue himself from a wanted felon. To be fair, I guess all of that is true, but this whole thing is too weird for me. I mean, had Mannie not actually been a zombie, I suppose it's possible the guy could have gotten away.

The story was, the guy was a wanted criminal in multiple states. Perhaps knowing that his time was coming, the perp robbed a bank and—when things went south—decided to take a hostage as a last-ditch effort to try to avoid jail and/or death by cop. As luck would have it, if you can call it luck, Mannie was nearby as the douchebag made his getaway. So Mannie ended up in the front seat of the bank robber's mustang, speeding along the Tennessee highways for almost six hours, until Mannie attacked the robber and nearly got them both thrown over a cliff.

It feels weird to say, but I was really, really rooting for that cliff. Then again, knowing my luck, Mannie would have survived the fall and caused even more trouble by being airlifted to a hospital or something. I can't imagine people explaining how Mannie could crash a medical helicopter, but I've been underestimating people's capacity to explain away Mannie's strange behavior this whole time, so it's possible they might not even blame him for that.

I'm in a restaurant now. Actually, to be more specific, I'm in the Nashville branch of the Tasty Train. I have to hand it to Mannie: the franchise is solid. Not that I love the train motif, but this restaurant is very much the same as its Las Vegas sister. The menu is slightly different, featuring native Tennessee cuisine like fried okra, but the servers are all dressed as train engineers and speak in the same insufferable puns. That said, the Tennessee employees seem a little more enthusiastic about the train lingo, which actually makes it more fun. Tell the truth, Tasty Train is kind of growing on me. For kicks, I've ordered some food I've never tried before: fried green tomatoes, okra, catfish, and a heaping helping of banana pudding for dessert. I've also asked for a side salad with no dressing, which earned me a raised eyebrow from the nice young waitress. I explained to her that I'm from California and am unused to the heavy food in the South, which made her laugh.

If you haven't already guessed, I haven't dated much. Call it a self esteem issue, but I've been reluctant to force my bullshit on anyone else. That, and I don't much care for dating. The whole thing makes me nervous: the questions, trying to eat and talk and still look attractive to someone. I guess you can go to movies, but then there's no getting to know each other. Besides all that, I'm a twenty-five-year-old fry cook, and a high school dropout townie to boot. Girls my age want someone who's got their act together, not some skinny punk kid who still lives with his mom.

Still, as I've been out traversing the greater United States, I've noticed women responding to me more positively than I'm used to. In this part of our vast country, I'm somewhat more exotic than I was in my go-nowhere northern California hometown, where blue hair is actually not that strange. When these Southern women hear I'm from California and look at my piercings, they think I'm someone who matters, or at least someone with an interesting story to tell. And the way they respond to me, I'm starting to feel like maybe they're right. Or maybe I'm carrying myself differently than I used to. I catch myself hunching a lot and make note to try to sit up straighter. I'm talking a little more confidently. Maybe being thrown in the deep end like this is having a positive effect on me after all. I'm definitely not as withdrawn and snappy as I usually am.

As I sit alone in my Tasty Train booth, watching the customers around me enjoy their food with company, I keep an eye on Mannie Fuego's table. People keep coming up to him and asking for autographs, and I try not to snort banana pudding out of my nose as I watch Mannie look at pens and notepads with hazy recognition. Actually, it's people's reactions to Mannie's attempt at signing autographs that really makes me bust up. It's all Mannie can do to hold the pen in one boxy fist and scribble on the paper. I heard one woman remark to her friend as they walked by my table that she thought maybe Mannie had a small stroke that went undiagnosed. It would certainly explain his erratic behavior and slack face.

For my own part, I can't bring myself to understand why Nashville's mayor brought Mannie Fuego to his own stupid restaurant. I can't explain exactly why, but doesn't that just seem like a weird move? Had it been me, I would've suggested going to a famous locally owned eatery. Mannie Fuego is some douchey restaurateur from California who opens franchises all over the country. Besides, wouldn't it be safe to assume Mannie's eaten at his own restaurant plenty? But I digress.

Mannie gets up from the table and wanders to the back, and the table presumes he's heading to the bathroom. One person notes that Mannie hasn't really touched his food and may not be feeling well. Personally, I'm grateful the restaurant is playing yacht rock just a touch too loud. (It just wouldn't be Mannie Fuego without the yacht rock.) It seems to be keeping Mannie in an exceptionally docile mood.

I'm only halfway through my food, but I slip out of my booth and sneak off after Mannie, wondering if this might be my chance. I doubt it, considering how loud a damn gunshot will be if I fire it off in the restaurant bathroom, but I refuse to let Mannie out of my sight.

I weave through a few tables, ignoring the glares from a group of older people and mutterings about millennials. One person wonders out loud to her dinner companions if I have a "real job." I mean, I kind of don't, but that isn't the point.

Ducking into the hallway at the back of the restaurant, I see Mannie amble past the bathroom and into the kitchen.

"Shit," I say, checking to make sure I've got my gun. If Mannie starts eating people in the kitchen, I'm going to have to open fire, right? I have to save people if Mannie starts attacking them. It's not like I can just let them die.

But I also don't have a concealed carry permit, and I can't for the life of me remember what Tennessee's gun laws are like. Based on stereotypes about the South, I assume maybe they're lax and it's cool for me to just be running around with a handgun in tow, but I really don't want to find out the hard way that what I'm doing is illegal.

Maybe I can grab a fire extinguisher and bash Mannie's head in with that?

My heart is racing, a fine sheen of sweat beading on my face and neck. My hands are shaking as I push the swinging gray doors and wander into the surgical brightness of the Tasty Train kitchen.

The kitchen crew greets Mannie enthusiastically, and I still can't figure out why it is that everyone is so into this guy. Maybe the cooks feel like they have to kiss Mannie's ass, since they technically—and I mean very technically—work for him?

"Hey Mannie!" an older man calls. "So good to have you. Thanks for coming back to say hello!"

Thinking fast, I take a couple of quick strides up to Mannie's side and stick my hand out to the gentleman. "Hey there, we're so glad to be here."

The man eyes me warily. "And who are you?"

"Oh!" I say, feigning embarrassment. My red face and general sweatiness must be helping my cause some, right? "I'm so sorry. I'm Mannie's assistant, Garrett."

Garrett is my best friend back home. I've got to come up with better aliases if I'm going to start giving people fake names. I'd make a really shitty secret agent.

The man sheds his skeptical expression and says, "Oh, great to meet you, Garrett! I didn't realize—"

"Yeah," I say, not letting him finish. "I'm fairly new. I'm so sorry we didn't contact you ahead of time."

"Quite alright," the man says, still shaking my hand. "I'm Frank, the general manager. We're just so pleased to have Mannie here tonight."

Mannie looks at me, his eyes dead, face slack. His jaw is hanging open, slightly askew, and I start to sweat more. Maybe it's because I know what Mannie is that his gaze makes me nervous, and I'm so grateful that the music is fairly loud back here too. I have to get Mannie the hell out of here, though. This is my chance.

"Hey Frank, I'm so sorry. Mannie has some pictures back in his trailer, and I know he'd love to give some to the kitchen crew. Which way to the back parking lot?"

A waiter pops into the back to drop an order, and I can feel the kitchen crew hesitating to get back to work. It's a busy night, after all, and the Tasty Train franchise operates like a well-oiled machine.

"In fact," I say, really leaning on my opportunity, "maybe we can stick around and do a more formal meet and greet after closing? I know that would make Mannie happy."

Mannie is still looking at me, but as he hears his name again, he nods slowly and claps his hands a couple of times. Out of the corner of my eye, it looks like maybe he's trying to smile. Maybe being back in a kitchen in his own franchise is bringing some humanity back to Mannie, resurfacing some genuine happiness in his cloudy consciousness. I'd give anything to know what—if anything—Mannie is actually thinking right now.

"That's a great idea," Frank says. "If you just go out that door there, you'll get to the back lot. You're sure you're okay to stay that late, Mister Fuego? I know you're a busy man."

To my great surprise, Mannie nods at Frank, and I feel a hard stab of guilt, which I force myself to ignore. I'm ready to get this over with, to make things right and head back home. All the fried food and barbecue I've been eating, on top of the stress, I've probably shaved a good five years off of my life already.

"Great. We'll see you later, Frank," I say, taking Mannie by the shoulders and steering him through the kitchen and out the back door.

It's quiet out here, and I can feel Mannie's mood shift immediately.

"Shit," I say. "You're hungry, aren't you, asshole?"

Mannie wrenches himself out of my grip, drool falling in big stringy chunks from his wide-open mouth.

I draw my gun but realize how close we are to the kitchen. Even with the silencer, I'm concerned about sound, so I do the best thing I can think of and sing the first song that comes to mind.

"Carry on my wayward sooooon," I croon. Mannie's expression immediately softens.

"There'll be peace when you are dooooone," I continue, taking Mannie by the shoulders and ushering him around the dumpsters. The back parking lot is empty, clearly a spot favored only by restaurant employees and people who need overflow parking. A single light hangs over the dumpster area, and I wish I had the guts to shoot it out. Instead, I usher Mannie into a shadowy spot, protected from view on one side. I take a look around for cameras, passersby, or people in their cars. It's empty. Blissfully empty.

Singing the guitar solo in a slightly off-key series of "duh nuh nuhs," I make sure my gun is loaded and the safety is off. I can hear the blood pounding in my ears, and I swear if I was any more nervous, my heart would explode. Mannie is standing against the wall, and suddenly we're doing a poor facsimile of an old western execution. I take a few steps back and take aim.

"Sorry Mannie," I say, putting my finger on the trigger.

The sound of glass shattering at my feet almost sends me into a full-blown panic. Snapping my head down and to the left to see what it is, I catch the distinct aroma of piss but have no time to process what has happened.

"Bradley Thomas Whittaker, you put that gun right down!"

"Wha—" I start, looking over my shoulder. Without warning, Mom barrels into me, knocking the gun out of my hand. It hits the ground and fires. I drop, scraping up the side of my face. By the time I'm back on my feet, Mannie Fuego is gone.

* * *

Mannie Fuego always dreamed of being rescued from a violent death.

It had been so nice to visit the Tasty Train restaurant, though Mannie found himself wondering when the food had gotten so bad. Nobody wanted to know this about Mannie, but he actually didn't really much care for trains. He said the "tasty train" catchphrase on *Mannie Fuego's Guide to Good Eats* a few times and it stuck. So, when it came time for Mannie to open his chain restaurants, the PR team decided that the train theme was the way to go.

Still, after all of his adventures, being in the Nashville Tasty Train felt a little bit like coming home. Plus, everyone in the restaurant loved him, which was nice, and they played his favorite music, because it turns out there isn't enough train themed music to stock a restaurant's running playlist. Still, they played "Locomotion" at his restaurants more than Mannie would have liked.

Sitting with his new friends at dinner, Mannie kept hoping someone would come by and bring him something better to eat than fried tomatoes and okra and all these other bready foods. Mannie wasn't sure what he was in the mood for, so he eventually got fed up and decided to go back to the kitchen to see what the deal was and if he might be able to special order something.

Mannie was having difficulty understanding the conversation with the people in the back, which he assumed was because his blood sugar was low. That's why it came as such a great surprise when one of his new friends—or was this blue-haired kid a fan? He seemed familiar—took him out back and aimed a gun at him.

Now Mannie is running, or doing his best to run, hoping to get as far away from the loud, scary gunshot as he can. In truth, it is really all Mannie can do to lope along—damn low blood sugar!

CHAPTER FOURTEEN

Chicago, Illinois

That night, in the abandoned parking lot behind the Nashville Tasty Train, Mom and I proceed to have one of the worst fights we have ever had.

"What the fuck, Mom?" I ask, back on my feet and dabbing fingers at the blood and grit embedded in my face, wincing at the pain. Everything happened so fast, it's taken me a minute to process. "Did you throw a jar of piss at me?"

But Mom was having none of it. "You were going to shoot him! Just shoot him in cold blood! I didn't raise you like that, Bradley! Your father and I didn't—" She takes a painful breath, choking on a sob, but I can tell that her tears are tempered with rage. "You lied to me, Bradley. You didn't even try to save him, you just marched him out here and decided to shoot him! Why didn't you try, Bradley, why—"

I've hit my limit with Mom's hysterics. "I didn't try because there is no goddamn spell to make zombies human again! There's literally nothing to try!"

Of course, she isn't satisfied with my answer. "Then why lie, Bradley? You shouldn't have—"

"You didn't leave me much of a choice!" I fire back. "You were freaking the fuck out, kind of like you are now, begging me to try something to make him human again. What the hell was I supposed to do?"

"I'm an adult, Bradley," she scolds. "You could have told me the truth. I would have made my peace with it."

"Really, Mom? You want me to believe you would have taken that kind of news in stride? Frankly, I've been walking on eggshells this entire time, trying to keep you from losing your shit because you finally left the house. How the fuck do you expect me to treat you like an adult when you can't even go out to buy groceries?"

I'm seething, out for blood. My words are sharp and I mean them to be. I'm sick of Mom's bullshit—sick of her hiding behind her fucking mood disorder to avoid living, to avoid anything that makes her remotely uncomfortable. This whole thing with Mannie could have ended tonight, but because of her childishness, Mannie Fuego has slipped away from us again. I want her to feel just as angry and tired and hurt as I am. I want her to know what her agoraphobia has done to me. I want her to know in no uncertain terms that Mannie getting away is her fault. I want her to feel guilty and stupid and ashamed, to apologize and beg for my forgiveness.

We all get this ridiculous when we're truly angry, don't we? I hope we do, otherwise I'm gonna be embarrassed.

Days pass, but we're still barely speaking to each other. I'm ashamed of the things I said but still too angry about losing Mannie to really apologize. So we're on the road, stuck in the truck together in this heavy silence. When we stop for food, Mom will somewhat perfunctorily give me her food order, almost as though she's taking pains to say as absolutely little as possible. It's times like these when I'm most tempted to just break down and apologize. Then I realize I've had to stop and buy new clothes every other day and take whore baths in restaurant sinks for days now. My back is full of knots and cricks because I've been sleeping in a fucking truck.

Pop-pop, bless his heart, is trying to mend fences. He didn't hear the fight (or claims he didn't) and keeps trying to draw the two of us into conversation. It's kind of him, but I feel like Mom and I need to work this out in our own time.

Mannie, the luckiest zombie in history, has been making his way north, weaving back west a little bit until he hit a straight trajectory into Illinois. Last I saw him, he was on the Sky Deck in Willis Tower, smiling that gape-mouthed smile he's been doing since he … well, died. On the Facebook post, he's crammed into the middle of a family of tourists—complete with fanny packs—and the lot of them appear to be suspended in thin air over the entire city. Of course, they're not; they're in some kind of insane bulletproof plexiglass, but I rather enjoy the effect. It's definitely a cool idea.

We arrived in Chicago a few hours ago, and I've been wandering the area around Willis Tower with no luck. Mannie's been quiet on social media for a while, so searching the streets is my best option. This part of Chicago is so thick with tourists, I feel like if Mannie popped up, there would be a crowd gathered around him.

Mom and Pop-pop are parked in a little lot over near the river, which I'm using to navigate the city. Well, that and the GPS map on my phone, of course. Still, the river is a fair enough point of reference that I don't find myself getting lost and needing to consult my phone as often as I've had to in other cities.

Chicago is a lively city, and I'm actually kind of enjoying walking around looking for Mannie. Not that this is a vacation by any stretch of the imagination, but the city is a good change of pace. I'm not usually into buildings, but the skyscrapers here have a really artistic feel. Just looking at them, I can tell that some date back to the depression, while others are definitely more modern. It makes me wish I knew anything about architecture, because I know I'd appreciate them as more than just aesthetically pleasing set pieces in the city. There's history here that I'm missing out on.

The day wears on and I'm getting hungry, so I start to keep an eye out for anyone who is selling Chicago-style hot dogs. For some reason, I imagined the city would have a hot dog vendor on every corner. This makes me wonder what preconceived notions people head into San Francisco with. Then again, I think San Francisco might a) have earned those preconceived notions, and b) will fulfill tourists' curiosity to get that real San Francisco experience and then some, so there's that.

I've wandered quite a ways, and I'm near the giant shiny bean when it hits me: I should get some deep dish. Mom's always wanted to try it too. Maybe bringing her some authentic Chicago-style deep dish will help us start talking.

But where to go?

I spot a tour guide leading a group of people off a waiting bus and can hear her as I approach.

"...back here by 3 pm, but until then, please feel free to explore and enjoy the park!"

The tourists disperse, and I approach her. She has a friendly face and wears her sandy hair tucked into a ball cap that designates her as a tour guide with a local company.

"Excuse me," I say. "I'm sorry to bug you. I know I'm not with the tour, but I'm looking for some good authentic deep dish. Do you have a suggestion?"

"Oh sure," she says, pointing back toward the river. "Just about a block that way you can stop by Giordano's. Best deep dish in the city."

A local man passing by overhears her and stops. "Don't listen to her, son. You want Lou Malnati's."

The woman insists. "I always suggest Giordano's. No one is ever disappointed."

The man scowls. "Lou Malnati's is the original—"

The argument escalates, but I've stopped listening. I head toward the river and spot Giordano's because there's a line out the door.

"Great," I say, heading to the line and claiming my spot. I'm hungry, but I also don't want to chance walking farther to Lou Malnati's. It's a good time to cruise around online and see if anyone else has run into Mannie.

I've been standing around Giordano's waiting for pizza for an hour when I finally get a hit on Mannie. A guy and his girlfriend have taken a cheesy selfie on the river, and a few people back, staring off at nothing in particular, is Mannie.

"Look whose inline for the boat tour with us!" the caption reads. The man's poor grasp of grammar grates on me.

"Large deep dish for Bradley," calls a woman at the counter.

"Great timing," I say as I slap down my receipt and swipe my pizza. I bolt out of Giordano's and mentally prepare myself to run three blocks with an extra large pizza.

Of course, people are giving me looks as I scramble to the river, but my haste is worth it. Running down the stairs to the river walk, I'm screaming, "Hold the boat, hold the boat!"

A few of the riverboat's crew members are looking at me strangely, and I realize that there's no one waiting in line. Is everyone on the boat already?

When I get close enough, one of the crew members—a younger man—approaches and asks, "You looking to take the river tour?"

"Yeah." I'm panting, and I'm sure I look and sound like a crazy person. "I want to get on the tour with Mannie Fuego."

"Oh," another crew member, a younger woman, speaks up. "Mannie's across the way with the other company."

She's pointing to a boat across the river which is—as we speak—just leaving the dock.

"Looks like you just missed him," the man says.

Across the river, I'm stress eating my fourth slice of Chicago deep dish and waiting impatiently for the boat to come back. After I finished throwing around every curse word I had ever heard, the crew of the Fair Lady Chicago Tours explained to me that the boat would be back in an hour.

That was almost exactly an hour ago, so I'm hoping to see the boat any minute now.

Like clockwork, the boat glides under one of Chicago's many bridges and begins to list back toward the dock on the opposite side of the river.

"What the fuck," I start, nearly dropping my pizza as I stand to get a better look. Running to the river's edge, I peer down at the boat and feel my stomach go to knots.

It's zombies. It's all zombies, with the exception—I think—of the captain, who's holed up in a tiny cabin and hastily guiding the boat back to the dock. The crew on the other side looks confused as the boat approaches but throws down a gangplank for the passengers all the same.

"No, don't!" I'm shouting, running for the bridge. "Don't let them off the boat! Shit shit shit!"

I'm regretting every day of P.E. I ditched in high school and the subsequent eight years of slovenly behavior that never, ever included running. Then again, even if I was a triathlete, I never would have gotten there in time to stop the horde from escaping onto Chicago's famous river walk.

That was the beginning of the end.

* * *

Mannie Fuego always dreamed of being invited to the White House.

Things in Chicago had been great, but at one point, things got a little hairy. People were screaming a lot. Mannie didn't like that at all.

He is wandering away from the more crowded parts of the city when someone pulls up beside him in a Winnebago and invites him to go to Washington, D.C. They say a lot of things about safety and the government. Mannie tries to explain that he isn't really into politics, but they pull him inside before he can protest.

CHAPTER FIFTEEN

Washington, D.C.

There were too many of them for me to stop.

I keep telling myself that. Even if I had started killing them, there would still have been too many. They got off the boat and scattered, agitated and eager to feed. I was still halfway across the goddamned bridge as they disembarked and ate the poor assholes with the My Lady of Chicago boat tours. I watched, horrified, trying to sing Toto to them, but I was too far away. The lively bands who played along the river earlier had dispersed as the sun got low in the sky. Without music, the zombies lost any shred of humanity they might have held, biting and tearing into the swaths of tourists crowded onto the river walk.

By the time I got there, Mannie Fuego was long gone. I fought my way through the crowd, trying to sing loudly enough to fend them off, but the virus spread through the crowd like wildfire. It was all I could do to get away before I was consumed by the chaos.

The news is out on the internet. Subreddits are freaking the fuck out, especially the ones dedicated to conspiracies. People are blaming the government or aliens. No one suspects an underachieving mid-twenties loser from a small town in California. Small blessings, I suppose.

I realize that, up until now, I've been just as lucky as Mannie in a way. Sure, he's eluded me at every turn, but I've managed to contain every litter of new zombies he's turned. I've managed to stay just one step behind him, cleaning up the messes he makes—until now.

"What the fuck do we do now?" I say, cradling my head in my hands. Mom's driving, one hand on the wheel as she chews on a piece of cold deep dish. This is the first time she's driven and eaten at the same time, and it's strange to see.

"Well, Bradley," she says through a mouthful of cheese and sauce, "we do what we've been doing. We follow Emmanuel, and when we catch up with him, you stop him."

"You make it sound so simple," I say through my palms.

"That's because it will be. Think about it: what's stopped you until now?"

"Um…" I sit up and lean back in my seat, staring at the ripped up cloth ceiling. "Mannie's inexplicable good luck?"

"And?" she coaxes.

"Fear that people will think I've murdered Mannie Fuego in cold blood like some kind of psychopath?"

"Exactly," Mom says with a smile. "And now, with the zombie apocalypse unfolding around us, you don't have to worry about that!"

"That is such a weird but good point," I say, furrowing my brows at the sagging cloth above me. "I can just shoot him now, the minute I see him."

"That's right, son," Pop-pop chimes in. "You're getting to be a pretty good shot, too. Shouldn't be too hard for ya. It's not like Mannie is all that fast."

Hope blooms in me, replacing the cold misery that had taken root somewhere in my chest and stomach.

"See Bradley? It's all going to be okay," Mom says, taking her eyes off the road to give me an encouraging smile.

Her kindness only rekindles the guilt I've been dragging around since our fight. "Mom, I'm really sorry for all those things I said back in Tennessee. That wasn't fair. It wasn't okay."

Mom takes a deep breath and turns her eyes back to the road. We've somehow gotten out of Chicago before the highways clog up, and we're making decent time on our way to D.C.

Mannie is riding there with a thirty-seven-year-old Chicago native named William and his two dogs, Peanut and Bruiser. I know a lot more about William, like the fact that he voted for Jill Stein and thinks that vaccines cause autism, because William's Facebook privacy settings are literally nothing. He has no privacy settings. I've looked through fifteen photo albums, primarily featuring him fishing with his dogs, a chocolate lab and a pit bull mix. (Plot twist: the pit bull is named Peanut and the chocolate lab is named Bruiser!) I guess I should be grateful; I've gotten this far on the good graces of people who feel the need to overshare.

William is live posting his flight from Chicago to D.C. as though he's hoping to go viral and become internet famous as the world is ending around him. Ugh, there I go again. Thanks for sharing, William. You're a true hero. William says he found Mannie by chance as he was driving out of town and had to save his second favorite celebrity. (His first favorite is Kim Kardashian, for reasons I can't ascertain by combing his social media accounts.)

William believes that D.C. will be safe because "Government officials are there and have a series of secret bunkers under the city for just such an emergency."

I mean, it's actually a fairly cogent idea, with the exception that if the government has secret apocalypse bunkers under the city, they most certainly aren't letting some mid-thirties bartender, his dogs, and a D-list celebrity in. I'm not sure what William is imagining is going to happen when they get there—if he can survive his trip east with Mannie in the first place—but he's in for a rude awakening.

"Bradley," Mom finally says. She's been quiet for a while, perhaps processing my apology, thinking of the right thing to say so we don't go right back to fighting.

"Yeah, Mom?"

"I'm sorry, too. And not just for this mess with Mannie. I'm sorry for—for not being there for you. You needed your mother, and I just hid ... I hid in plain sight."

"Mom, don't. I'm really sorry," I say and mean it.

"No, Bradley, I need to apologize for this. I know I can't help if my brain is wired wrong, but I should have fought it. I should have kept going to therapy, even if it scared the hell out of me to leave the house. Even if I got there shaking and sweating, I should have fought it every goddamned day until it got better. Heck, even if it never got better, I should have kept fighting. But I didn't do any of that. I laid down. I gave up." Quiet tears are falling down her cheeks. "I let you finish raising yourself, and when you dropped out of school, I let you, because who was I to tell you to face something that scared you when I refused to do the same?

"But you know what? This whole adventure, it's been good for me. I'm getting better. I mean"—she laughs a little—"I was out of the truck the night I threw that jar of pee at you! That's the farthest I got from the truck so far: forty whole feet!"

"So far?" I ask.

Mom blushes. "I've been forcing myself to take little excursions from the truck. It was kind of ... necessary once I realized I could only pee in jars."

"Oh Jesus, thank you so much for not shitting in jars, Mom," I say earnestly. "Wait, so that jar of piss you threw at me was—?"

"Yeah, that was from me. I've been keeping them behind the driver's seat." Mom's red, her eyes on the road.

That's fucking sick, but I don't say as much. Instead, I focus on the positive. "I'm really proud of you, Mom. That must have been hard, leaving the truck."

"It was," Mom said. "It is. But if I take baby steps, I know I can keep getting better."

I nod, and a comfortable silence settles over us.

"Mom?" I ask after a while.

"Yeah, Bradley?"

"Can I ask you something?"

I kind of hate when people say that, but I at least understand the motivation. And now, I'm nervous to ask. We've been so honest with each other, and I need to know. I've been hanging on to this question for over a decade.

"How long did you and Pop-pop know Dad was sick?"

Mom frowns. "A few months."

"And why—" My voice cracks, which is really fucking embarrassing. "Why didn't anyone tell me?"

Mom looks over at me, fresh tears in her eyes. "We all had different reasons. Looking back, I know now that none of them were good. I can't imagine how it felt, finding your father like that."

"I kept thinking, had I only known, I could have done something. Or Pop-pop—"

Pop-pop's voice is gentle as he says, "The Gift doesn't work that way, son. Even I won't live forever in this goddamn chair. And even if we could have put him in a chair, or a lamp, your father wouldn't have wanted to live that way. I don't think you would have liked it either. Being trapped in living room furniture is no way to live, especially not when you've got a young boy to look after."

Mom chimes in. "We wanted you to enjoy the last of your time with him without the burden of knowing that it was the last of your time with him. Sometimes, I wish I had the same luxury. Instead, I spent months wondering if everything was our last. Our last weekend breakfast, our last trip to the city, our last stupid movie. I was so wrapped up in my fear of when we might lose him that ... I don't know, those months just slipped by."

It was only after Dad had been dead for several years that I began to put the pieces together. He was losing hair, but I was eleven and assumed that's just what happened to dads. Sometimes, he was sick or too fatigued to do one of our normal things like go to the park and play stickball, but he hid it well. He bought us a Gamecube, and we spent more time together on the couch. I thought nothing of it. I just figured my dad was cool and liked video games. I'm so fucking stupid.

Mom wipes a fresh tear from her cheek. "Bradley, there are a lot of things I should have done differently. A lot of things I wish I had done differently. The thing no one tells you about being an adult is that you'll stumble through it just as bewildered and confused as you've stumbled through everything else. We only look like we have it all together because we've gotten better at hiding how completely panicked we are… And even then, sometimes things come along and knock you right down. I wasn't ready to face life without your father. I didn't know how. But I'm sorry all the same, because I should have gotten up and tried."

"Stop apologizing, Mom," I say. She's beating herself up just as badly as I beat myself up. All at once, I realize this is a learned behavior, and we don't have to keep living in this cycle of bullshit.

D.C. is a war zone.

Every available fighting body is in the streets, and the city is in a declared state of emergency. People are holed up in their homes, and many of them have boarded up the doors and windows. It's funny, I always expected people to panic and flee in situations like this, but the media has managed to spin the story and keep people inside. Frankly, that's probably safer than people running in every direction.

The city is actually taking refugees from other places and has a triage set up to welcome them in. If Mannie Fuego is in D.C., he would have passed through here. Someone would have had to detain him, right? I haven't seen an update from Winnebago William in three hours, which concerns me.

We're ushered through a mandatory checkpoint, and I sense my chance.

A National Guard soldier approaches our truck as Mom stops and rolls down the window (literally rolls, because our truck is just that old).

"Good evening, Ma'am, Sir," the soldier says, reflecting us back at ourselves in his oversized aviator sunglasses. "Where you from?"

"Chicago," I say hastily. No need to raise suspicion by saying we're from California. There's no way we could have gotten that far since the breakout in Chicago. "We're looking for shelter. All we could grab from our home before we had to run was my mother's favorite armchair."

Our story is apparently just sad enough to warrant a minuscule head nod from the guardsman. We're asked to step out of the car and into a small tent, where we are impersonally checked for bites, scratches, or any signs of zombie tampering. Once cleared, we're sent on our way to the refugee shelter.

"You folks are lucky," the soldier says before we drive away. "Mannie Fuego is supposed to be at that shelter."

* * *

Mannie Fuego never wanted to have to stay in an evacuation center.

It is crowded and loud, and people keep asking him if he'd like to cook for the other evacuees. Why would Mannie cook anything? People seem to forget that Mannie is really only good at eating other people's cooking and tossing catchphrases around.

In truth, Mannie is sad that he has not—in fact—been summoned to Washington, D.C., to meet the president and receive some sort of medal for being great. Instead, Mannie's new friend—whose name he never got—seemed to only be interested in finding this awful shelter. Mannie isn't sure why. Things are much more exciting in the city, what with the tanks and helicopters and whatnot.

Mannie sure wishes he had come up with a catchphrase that involved cooler vehicles than trains.

After a group of hipsters bust out some acoustic guitars and sing Beatles covers, Mannie decides he needs to leave the shelter in search of something to eat. The shelter food is miserable and definitely isn't going to get him anywhere near the Tasty Train. Hell, why didn't Mannie think to say "Tasty Tank" instead? His life would have been so much better that way.

C H A P T E R   S I X T E E N

Washington, D.C. (Still)

I have acquired a series of items that allow me to pass through the city in almost dubious safety.

Mom and Pop-pop are at the evacuation center. The Red Cross wouldn't let Mom bring Pop-pop in, so she's staying in the truck. To be honest, I doubt she would go in even if they let her take Pop-pop. Just because she can get forty feet from the truck doesn't mean she can suddenly handle an evacuation center in the midst of a zombie apocalypse.

I went into the center, and I'm ashamed to admit that I had to steal a few things to create the system I've got now: a little red wagon loaded with Bluetooth speakers, which I have synced to my phone. As you might expect, 5G coverage is spotty, and my Pandora station is stuck on the ironic dance mix I made specifically for when I play first-person shooters. Not only that, but because the 5G coverage is going in and out, the station is stuck on "We Like to Party." I've been wandering around Washington, D.C., hearing about how the Vengabus is jumpin' over and over again. If only happiness was just around the corner.

Fortunately, the zombies I encounter seem to like the song just fine and pass me by like I'm just another one of them. There's much less military presence in this part of the city, north of the White House. As can perhaps be expected, the majority of the ground troops are gathered around the White House and the Pentagon. Here, residents have been left to fend for themselves, and I see people peering at me from upper-level windows as I wander by with my mobile DJ booth.

I know where I'm going because news helicopters have spotted Mannie in passing. He's wandering around the Smithsonian National

Zoological Park. Finally, his limited mental capacity is working in my favor: he seems to be trapped. The park is also full of zombies, so no one is bothering to stage a rescue. I'm not shocked to learn that no one has figured out that Mannie is part of the undead masses wandering the zoo. It just fucking figures at this point.

My thoughts are interrupted by the suspicious absence of late 90's Europop.

"The fuck," I say, looking at my phone. No service. Nothing.

I look up. I'm maybe a quarter of a mile from the zoo's entrance. The only thing between me and the gate is a somewhat disheveled parking lot. A couple of zombies are eyeing me, perhaps trying to determine whether or not I'm one of them. God, what I wouldn't give to hear the Venga Bus's horn right now. I know there's really only one thing I can do to safely make it into the zoo.

I slip my phone into my pocket, drop my little red wagon's handle, and book it the fuck across the parking lot.

If I make it through this alive, I'm going to take up running. You know, just in case this happens again.

As I launch myself across the parking lot, I'm belting as loud as I can, "I'VE GOT SOMETHING TO TELL YA! I'VE GOT NEWS FOR YOUUUUU…"

Because I've heard the song thirty times on loop, I know literally every word and instrumental break of the song. It's the only thing in my head, so I sing it. I belt it. I give it feeling, as though I truly want the undead wanderers around me to know that I like to party. Still, my range isn't great, and I have a narrow miss as an aggro old lady zombie grabs at my shirt with her massive acrylic talons. Seriously, why does anyone do their nails like that, anyway? I elbow her in her wrinkled face and pick up the pace, bracing myself to hop and slide across the hood of a Mustang that's stuck in my way—you know, Dukes of Hazzard style.

It does not work out. The ass of my jeans is clammy, and I slide a bit, roll a bit, and end up eating shit on the pavement. My teeth go through my tongue and I scream as blood floods my mouth. Seeing zombie feet converging on me, I force myself to keep singing even as my tongue is swelling. The feet stop, giving me a moment to pick myself up and keep running.

When I get to the zoo's gate, I'm winded and still not through the woods. The park is overrun, and I start to wonder if I'm actually going to survive this.

As if answering my thoughts, a truck rolls into view, being driven clumsily by a zombie. Finally, all those hours playing Grand Theft Auto are going to pay off. Thinking fast, I run up to the slow-moving truck, wrench the door open, and haul the driver out. Using the door and back of the driver's seat, I hoist myself in and slam and lock the door as I press my foot to the brake.

"Oh thank fuck Jesus god damn," I pant, reaching for the radio dial. Static greets me on every channel but one, and as the familiar notes hit me, I start to laugh—not gently, like someone who has enjoyed a decent joke, but hysterically, like someone who's spent the past week and a half trying to put down the zombie apocalypse and is laughed at by God at every turn. I guess I'm finally ready to laugh with him.

Still laughing, I roll the windows down and crank the music up. The park's zombies mellow out to the smooth synthy sounds of Toto.

I drive slowly around the park blasting D.C.'s inexplicably still running 80's radio station, eyes peeled for Mannie. With there being one bottleneck entrance and exit from this zoo and no actual humans left to escort him out, I know he's here. Call me crazy, but I can feel it.

I spot him stuck on an ice rink. I hop out of the truck but leave the key turned in the ignition so the music keeps going. Mannie spots me as I approach, and I'm surprised as I set foot on the rink. It isn't ice. Fake snow settles in my hair and blasts itself all over the rink. I guess D.C. doesn't get cold enough for an honest to goodness ice skating rink, which doesn't really make sense to me because my grasp of geography is miserable. Gun to my head, I would have told you it snowed here.

Mannie is swaying gently to the music as I step cautiously across the rink, fumbling for my gun. Pulling it from its concealed holster—I'm pretty sure concealed carry is illegal in the capital, but fuck it, zombie apocalypse—I take the safety off and aim.

"This is it, Mannie," I say, wondering if he understands. Hoping he does. "I do feel like I owe you an explanation though," I sigh. All around us, zombies are moving in, drawn to the music eddying from the truck. Some have stopped to sway—as Mannie does—to the easy beats.

"I'm sorry, Mannie. I gave you bad beef. This whole thing is my fault, and now you've gotta die so everything else can go back to normal." My finger is poised on the trigger in case he makes any sudden moves. I'm not letting him get away again.

"And you know, despite everything you've put me through, in some ways I'm still not ready to kill you. I mean, don't get me wrong. I used to think you were a total douchebag. I guess I still do in a lot of ways. But over the past few days, I've gotten to see all of these crazy things all over the country. I've eaten at two of your restaurants and had all of this amazing local cuisine. All my life I've been stuck in this tiny town—that shithole where you ate the bad burgers—and I never realized exactly how much I've been missing. I've always been afraid to put myself out there, I guess. But you, I mean... You are a stupid, talentless blowhard with really, really outdated hair, but you put yourself out there anyway. You do your show and eat people's food and say your dumb catchphrase and get to do all these amazing things. All because you had the courage to do it, because you weren't afraid of failing, I guess. Or, I don't know, if you were, you didn't let it get you down.

"I guess what I'm trying to say is"—I take a deep breath and let it out slowly, my index finger putting just the barest pressure on the trigger—"I've kind of come to respect you. Hell, in a fucked up way, I actually admire you."

★ ★ ★

Mannie Fuego always dreamed of meeting his biggest fan...

Back in that Small Town in Northern California

Nobody remembers what happened. Well, nobody except myself, Mom, and Pop-pop.

As we drove back home, it was as though the entire United States was waking up from a strange dream. No one was reported missing or dead. Somehow, the same magic I used to fuck everything up had the power to set everything straight. And I mean everything.

So the only real casualty of all of this is my enduring lack of motivation.

No, you read that right. Mannie Fuego is still alive.

I remember squeezing the trigger, imagining Mannie Fuego's head as a giant fluorescent red tin can, and just feeling so ready for everything to go back to normal. The gun fired with a loud crack, and I felt this weird sense of relief. The zombified people all dropped to the ground.

For a moment, I just stood there and stared at Mannie's body. Relief be damned, I meant what I said to him. And I hated that he'd died because of me.

I slow-shuffled across the ice and crouched beside him. Maybe it was desperation. Maybe it was because I was alone. But I said the words Pop-pop had encouraged me to say. You know, the nonsense ones.

"Imorium nyros. Imorium nyros. Imorium nyros. Come on, Mannie, I know you can do this. You tricked the entire country into believing you weren't dead. There's something inside you, still. Even now. So please, just..."

I felt the magic start to leave my body, just like it did when I freshened up potatoes. So I imagined Mannie as one big, giant, fatally wounded potato. I wiped my hand across the bullet wound, closed my eyes, and begged whatever power existed in the universe—in ME—to make Mannie fresh again.

Eyes pinched shut hard I admit, "You don't deserve to die for my fuckup."

Mannie groaned. Not like a zombie. Like a person waking up with a bad hangover.

"Holy shit, dude, that was some party."

I took off running, barely managing to avoid biffing it on the ice. All around me, people were waking up.

Mannie quit doing Mannie Fuego's Guide to Good Eats and left the Food Network altogether. I heard a rumor he's selling off the Tasty Train franchise, too.

"I wanna like, see the world and do cool stuff," Mannie said in a recent interview, tipping his sunglasses up to wince into the camera for a second. "So I'm proud to be working with Bravo to bring you Mannie Fuego's Hot Travel Tips!"

Mom's delighted. I'm glad she's happy, but you'll excuse me if I end my adventures with Mannie here.

The first thing I did when we got back home was check on Uncle Bernie. He was none too happy to be locked up in the back room, but he survived the couple of days after coming back to his human self by eating canned food and—as you do—choosing a corner to shit in. I agreed to hire a cleaning company and pay for it out of my next, and last, paycheck.

Second, I gave Uncle Bernie my notice and asked how soon he'd let me leave. He admitted he had a stack of applications from high school kids who needed part-time work and sent me on my way.

"You're overqualified to be a fry cook anyway," Uncle Bernie said with a wave. "I can hire a couple of kids from the high school and pay them half what you're making."

It was the closest Uncle Bernie would get to saying "Go on, get out of here and make something of yourself" he would ever get.

If you're curious, the third thing I did was take the world's longest shower.

I've enrolled in classes at the junior college a few towns over and am living on my savings for now. I'm taking culinary classes, history, English, even a psych class. The JC even has a program for me to get my GED, which I've enrolled in. I don't know what I really want to do with myself yet, so I'm letting school inspire me. What I'm learning so far is that I have a lot of options and that a lot of stuff interests me.

Mom is sticking to her word and going back to therapy. Her recovery is definitely two steps forward and one step back, but we're getting close to being able to go out to our favorite Italian restaurant again. I call that progress for sure.

Pop-pop is teaching me a little bit more about my magic. I'm not sure I'll ever use it again, but I agree it's time I know what I'm capable of doing so that I never, ever accidentally make a mistake like the Wagyu Beef Incident ever again.

I wish I could tell you that I'm now making six figures and living it up, but I'm not. I'm still driving my Dodge Colt, still living with my mom and grandpa. I've got my own issues to work through after everything, too. But the one thing I can say for certain—the great positive to come out of all of this—is that I'm no longer standing still.

About the Author

Diana Gray, known as Ember in online spaces, is a Northern California native with a passion for writing everything from blogs to epic fantasy novels. Really, the only thing she doesn't like to write is biographies about herself.

To date, her published works include this novella, a whole mess of blog posts for clients and past employers, and her award-winning short story: *The White Sweater*. She is currently working on a three-book fantasy epic and the sequel to *Mannie Fuego's Guide to Good Eats*.

Her hobbies include playing video games and table-top RPGs, yoga, gardening, traveling, watching YouTube deep-dives into niche video game lore and pop culture drama, drawing, and making lists. She also owns and operates a small graphic design and media consulting business.

Diana lives in the picturesque Northern California mountains with her husband, their son, and their three very strange cats.